MW01235031

BEHIND HIS MASK

D. J. Coleman

iUniverse, Inc.
New York   Bloomington

BEHIND HIS MASK

Copyright © 2009 D. J. Coleman

This is a work of fiction. All of the characters, names, incidents,
organizations, and dialogue in this novel are either the products
of the author's imagination or are used fictitiously.

iUniverse books may be ordered through booksellers or by contacting:

iUniverse
1663 Liberty Drive
Bloomington, IN 47403
www.iuniverse.com
1-800-Authors (1-800-288-4677)

ISBN: 978-1-4401-3457-9 (pbk
ISBN: 978-1-4401-3458-6 (ebk)

Printed in the United States of America

iUniverse rev. date: 4/13/2009

*

**Dedicated to my best friend and brother
Mr. James Lee Jones**

August 25, 2000

Thank you for passing through my life.

*

Prologue

Reflections of how it all began...

A CANOPY OF SADNESS AND gloom filled Jackson's office as he crushed the wide selection of papers lying on his desk. Assorted pieces of multi-colored glass could be seen sifted throughout his shiny green finished marble floor. Enraged with hurt and pain, he released his aggression on the delicate collection of crystal vases and picture frames that once occupied the bookshelf behind his desk.

He reached over to the cherry finished end-table, and then he took another gulp of the *Chivas Regal Scotch* bottle he had been working on since arriving at the office. The image of a distraught and not so well groomed man is the image he saw as he surveyed himself in the mirror. His eyes fell on his college yearbook nestled mysteriously in the middle of the psychology journals, and bound periodicals he referred to often in his practice. A strange sense of Déjà Vu halted his alcoholic stupor long enough for him to grab his yearbook off of the shelf. He opened the yearbook and leafed through its pages as if it were the first time he'd seen it. Funny, he had no memory of putting the yearbook there. Even though he referenced that particular shelf many times, he never stumbled upon it before. Why now? And how under the circumstances was he able to see it all of a sudden? The rage and depression he had been experiencing caused him to finally see those items. Jackson found enough strength to make his way to the chair behind his desk so that he could review the yearbook.

He lifted the cover with apprehension, and then braced himself for the journey back to a time he almost forgot. He made his way through the book stopping only at the places that made a brief smile return to his face. Homecoming spilled out of the middle of the book, almost center fold style as Denise's picture reintroduced itself to him. *"Miss Terminus University"* hovered in a bold caption just above her bejeweled crown. At that moment, Jackson was webbed into the time warp that had him meeting Denise for the first time.

It all happened on a cool September day while Jackson and Denise were registering for the fall semester. The grounds were covered with yellow and orange leaves dampened by showers earlier that morning. The sky showed no signs of a ray of sunshine anywhere amongst the overcast charcoal colored clouds. However, in Jackson's mind when he entered the auditorium and laid eyes on Denise, he saw the sunshine he had been looking for. As he passed Denise in the registration line, she greeted him with a warm inviting smile. It was apparent that Denise had an instant interest for Jackson as well.

Denise was the president of her sorority, and she was recently crowned queen of *T.U.* that year. She had the right curves, the perfect smile, and the fullest set of jet-black shoulder length hair Jackson had ever seen. Enthralled by her beauty, Jackson's mind began its own journey unbeknownst to his conscious. But then the sudden boom of the clerk's voice shook him abruptly, allowing him to return quickly to his present reality. "Boy do you plan on registering today? Or will it be next week? I have to take my lunch soon, so you need to move along. I don't have all day," commanded the heavy set, blond streaked woman standing before him.

On the way home he rehearsed internally what he would say to Denise if he were ever to see her again. When he finally got back to his dormitory he headed straight for the shower. He would have to hurry in order to be ready for his fraternity's business meeting. As president of *Gamma Gamma Phi*, he had to be there to ensure everything on the agenda was addressed. The brothers had a lot to cover such as new probates, and their annual charity event, which was coming up next month.

As Jackson raced around his dorm room searching for his keys, the phone rang. It was no surprise to him that it was his mother. He realized he should have called her to let her know he arrived back to campus safely. Even though *Terminus University* was just forty-five minutes outside of Atlanta, she reserved her right to worry, and still kept a close watch on him. "I'd better make sure I call her later," he thought to himself. As he checked his watch, it confirmed his next thought that he was going to be late.

"Damn," he exhaled in his own disgust just as he gave the key its final twist in the lock. At that moment a guy brushed up against Jackson almost at the same rate of anxiousness. The mistake gave way to an arrogant "hello" from the stranger, but the encounter caused Jackson to drop his keys with the famed *"Gamma Gamma Phi"* shield dangling on the ring. In an effort to modify the mistake, the stranger immediately returned the keys to Jackson's hands. Without giving the stranger more attention than he deserved, Jackson shrugged off the encounter and hurried to his car. After all, it was just a careless bump from a stranger.

Minutes later he pulled up to the parking lot surrounding the student union building. Students were known for gathering casually around the building as they went to and from class. This was the meeting spot known to all as a place you could most likely be found if someone was looking for you. Another smile came across Jackson's face as he remembered how he was always rushing, and that day was no different. Not only was his pace rapid, but his heart thumped even harder than the rhythm of his steps as he walked on the yard. As his approach drew nearer to the student union, he realized that Denise was standing outside talking to her sorority sisters. Jackson found himself becoming very nervous as he walked over and asked Denise out on a date. Luckily Denise said yes, and so his natural reaction was to tell her that he would call her after his fraternity meeting. Jackson and Denise would soon enter into a world they both thought they could handle. However, in the years to come their relationship would manifest itself with more consequences than benefits.

He finally stopped reflecting on his college years and became sad again as he stared out of his office window at the deep dark-blue night sky. On that night there seemed to be no trace of a moon, or a star which could give him some light to his darkness. Jackson found himself alone, in despair as his mind took its own course down memory lane.

Chapter 1

THE WEEKEND WAS FINALLY HERE and I felt relieved knowing that now I could catch up on some much needed sleep. I have not been able to sleep for over a month now ever since I started working with a young girl by the name of Jacquelyn Matthews. I decided to leave my office at four o' clock, that way I could avoid the hectic traffic. I felt a cool fierce chill brush against my face when I stepped outside. That was an indication that the transition from fall to winter had already taken place. I came to this conclusion because I could see light drops of snow falling from the sky. I loved watching the snow fall from my bedroom window, while sipping a nice cup of hot coffee. Seeing the first flakes of the season reminds me of one of the reasons I moved here from the south. December was also my most favorite month of the year because of all the holidays and festivities.

My name is Dr. Jackson Eugene Phillips and this is the story of my life. New York City is a place where I found refuge after graduating from medical school and leaving my hometown of Atlanta, Georgia. I always said that if I could make it in the Big Apple then I could make it anywhere. It truly is the city that never sleeps, and whatever you can think of doing is here in New York. The busy sidewalks, the traffic, and the hustle and bustle have converted a country boy from Georgia into a city boy. After visiting New York a few times, I was inspired to move here and start my own private clinical practice. I always thought this would be a good place to start my life. I discovered during my junior year in undergrad, while doing my internship at a local counseling center, that I enjoyed counseling both children and adults. My career has its challenges I will admit, partly because I often find myself wanting to take on my client's problems. But I learned early on during my graduate studies not to bring my work home with me.

My two best friends Darren and Denise decided after years of debating to accompany me by moving here as well. The three of us knew that coming to New York would be a better opportunity for us to prosper in each of our careers and dreams. The irony of Denise and I becoming best friends at times astounds me. But at this point in the game how we landed here, I guess is just a small part of the story which is my life.

While I was walking to my car, a promoter alongside the street handed me a handbill for Gayle's Soul Food Restaurant. The handbill advertised that tonight there would be some spoken word, and live neo-soul singers performing. I stopped for a moment and reviewed the colorful handbill, and then I got in my car and headed straight home. To my luck traffic was not that bad, besides it only took me fifteen minutes to get home when traffic was great. My office was in Manhattan on East 35th Street. I lived in Strivers Row Harlem on Fredrick Douglas Boulevard, an upscale community with a population made up solely of upper class educated African-Americans. I chose this community after doing my own research and obtaining guidance from my broker Yolanda Banks. She and I met at my assistant Shelia's business social party a few months after I moved to New York. I discovered from Sheila that having house parties for black professionals was a big thing to do in the Upper East Side.

When I finally arrived home I laid my briefcase down and reached for a bottle of Civello Pinot Gris out of the refrigerator. I picked up this delicious wine last month when I attended a wine tasting festival in Greenwich Village on 8th street. I really was exhausted, but I took the time to sort through the massive pile of mail on the kitchen counter. I was glad to see that I had a postcard from my good friend

Eric Cartwright. Eric and I were fraternity brothers who met at our annual *Gamma Gamma Phi* convention years ago in Florida. He was an alumnus of *Bayard University,* a historically black college, which is also the place where our fraternity was founded. I recently visited the campus in Tennessee, and was very excited about meeting some of my other fraternity brothers on the campus. I admired the fact that Eric was also into politics and the entertainment business. He would always keep me up to date on what was current. As I was loosening my tie, I noticed the flashing red light, an indication that I had a few messages to review, blinking on my cell phone.

As I sat at the kitchen table I poured myself a glass of wine and checked each message. To my surprise, I had several messages from my sister Tonya, my mother, and my ex-fiancé Denise. I decided that I would call my mother later to see what she might have wanted. She was probably running my sister and her fiancé Brian crazy. Tonya was getting married soon, and so that meant my mother would be very busy preparing for her big day, not Tonya's. This is potential husband number three for Tonya. I started counting the men who would marry my sister after the second husband-to-be didn't. My mother had a way of always being overbearing in both of our personal lives. I have mastered not being so revealing to her about my personal life, partly because I now live in New York, so she can't just show up at my doorstep unannounced.

I immediately decided to give Denise a call instead to see what her plans were for the evening. We had not seen each other in weeks, and although we used to be engaged that still did not stop us from being close friends. I once dreamed that she and I would have a house in the country with a large wrap-around porch. I even envisioned that Denise and I would sit on the porch in the evenings together and watch the little ones run around as the sunset. However, that fairy tale came to an end years ago when I left her at the altar.

I remember that day as if it were yesterday. The weather was in our favor because the sun was shining. There was a crisp cool breeze to compliment the radiance of our union as well, but unfortunately in my mind all I could see was a cloud of darkness. I had some deep issues to confront and chose to call the wedding off after minutes of talking to myself in the mirror. Denise was hurt and wouldn't speak to me for months. Eventually she slowly came back into my life, and I vowed to never hurt her like that again. We will always have a lot of love for each other, but I don't think it's fair for me to be her husband right now. I have a lot of demons to deal with, and until I do that, I think being friends is best. When the time is right I will become more open with Denise, but the reality is the time may never actually be right. I dialed Denise and after two rings she picked up.

"Hello, can I speak to Foxy Crawford?" I asked as I tried not to laugh.

"Well only if three thousand dollars is paid first, and a pedicure appointment is setup."

"Well, I'll have to get back with you on that one. I see that you called me earlier?"

"Yes I did. Darren and I are going to this soul food joint called J.J.'s on 125th Street in Harlem, and we wanted to know if you wanted to hang out with us tonight?"

"That's sounds inviting. Ah, around what time are you and Darren planning on meeting up?"

"Maybe around seven or eight o' clock, but I can't stay out too late. I have a hair appointment in the morning, and then I have to meet with my stylist at noon. A Diva has got to get much sleep. I have a huge fashion presentation to prepare for," Denise boasted.

"I will take you up on your offer. But I will need to take a shower and freshen up. I've been in this suit all day and I need some air. You know I have to look and smell good," I said as I took off my shirt.

"Now I like to smell and see a good looking man from time to time. Hell, it kind of compliments my style when I'm in his presence. Let me stop," Denise laughed. "Oh before I forget, do you know how to get to J. J.'s?"

"Yeah I passed by it today on my way home. I started to go there tonight for dinner but changed my mind. However, when I was walking to my car this evening to head home, a promoter handed me a handbill about a place called Gayle's. The advertisement stated that tonight they will have Ron Deheem a new poet doing spoken word. I am in the mood for some jazz and poetry. What do you think about that place instead?"

"That sounds good! I did read an article about Gayle's and the review was excellent."

"Alright then, that sounds like a plan. Let Darren know, and I'll meet you both there at seven o' clock."

"Great! I can't wait to tell you and Darren about my latest new celebrity gossip. You will not believe the stuff I heard about that new singer Tracy. We'll talk over dinner."

"See there you go talking about people. Let me get off the phone before I get dragged into another one of your entertainment business gossip spells. Goodbye Denise..."

"Goodbye, Jackson", Denise giggled.

After talking to Denise I opened my wardrobe to the difficult choices involved with getting dressed. My final selection was to wear a coffee colored two-button blazer and some jeans. I decided to wear a matching scarf and hat as well. I started the shower and then placed my feet slowly into the bathtub to take a hot shower. The hot water performed its magic as I rocked my body back and forth allowing the hot water to massage my back and then my neck. You can always count on a hot shower to give your sore muscles the comfort you need. While I was in the mirror I realized as I was shaving that I was starting to age a little. I considered myself still a handsome man, but the way I looked ten years ago was not the reflection I saw in the mirror tonight. I rinsed my face with a hot towel and then I massaged my body all over with some coco butter. I finally got dressed, and then I gave myself one final review in the mirror. I grabbed my cell phone and my wallet, and then I raced out the door. As I was heading to the elevator Carrington the front desk guard from downstairs approached me.

"Good evening Dr. Phillips, I am glad I was able to catch you before you headed out. I have a package to deliver to you sir."

"What's this for?" I asked with a confused expression on my face.

"I'm not sure, Dr. Phillips. It came this morning. Since you didn't pick it up, I thought I would bring it upstairs to you."

"Well that was really nice of you," I said, pulling a bill from my pocket. "Thanks."

"Thanks, Dr. Phillips! Have a nice night."

Carrington was a new front desk guard in my building who worked the evening shift. His job was to greet the residents and make sure the premises were always secure. Carrington reminds me of myself when I was younger, so full of optimism and ambition. He is always very well groomed, well spoken, and a very polite person. I took a look at the package, contemplated opening it, and then realized that it was already six thirty. I would have to postpone reviewing it until later. I wanted to look at the package when I had more time. It probably was just something I ordered one night when I was bored. I have a tendency to go on online shopping sprees when I am bored or depressed. Food was once the filler of my emotional escapades, but I stopped that after I joined the gym and got myself a trainer. I had gained so much weight until Denise and Sheila would ask me what was wrong with me. So, to keep them out of my personal life which, remind you I have always done a good job of covering up, I decided to stop over eating. I took the box with me and headed to the elevator to leave when my neighbor Ms. Clara stopped me and informed me that she saw that I had a visitor twice today. When she asked this person what they wanted she said they just wanted to know if they had the right address. How this mysterious person was able to get past security is still a shock to me. But whatever they wanted I have a feeling they will be back.

Ms. Clara was one of the nosiest people I knew, so I am sure the next time this person stops by she will give me a better description and tell me what they wanted. I have to admit that at times Ms. Clara can be good as a watchman here for the residents. I remember she helped identify a robber who mugged one of the residents one night while she was getting out of the cab. It was a cold winter night and Mr. and Mrs. Banks were coming home from a gala. A guy came up behind Mrs. Banks and put a gun to her head demanding that she give him her purse. Later Ms. Clara testified in court about the incident and she was able to identify the mugger. Ironically the guy she testified against lived in our neighborhood. She remembered seeing him a few times when she would walk her dog. I found out through the other residents that she does not leave home without her friends Smith and Weston. I guess you could say the old lady wanted to be prepared in case she was next to get hit by a mugger.

I thanked her for informing me, and then I got in the elevator and proceeded to the car garage. I was very apprehensive about coming home by myself tonight, but I am quite certain that if Carrington suspects anything suspicious he will notify the authorities. After I got off the elevator, I looked behind me a few times while I walked to my car. A sinister feeling found its way all over my body as I drove off to meet Denise and Darren. One of the reasons I moved into this community is because I felt I could be safe. The reality is no matter where you go crime and dishonest people may show up. I am not sure if this mystery person is even a bad thing but then again you never know. My mind began to wonder if one of my clients found out where I lived. I didn't think that was possible, but there have been a few crazy people that I thought could be the person. To get my mind off of the mystery person and my long work week, I listened to some jazz. My mother, believe it or not, turned me on to jazz as a child. She told me that before she started singing at church she was a former jazz singer. So, through her educating me on the different styles of jazz and its composers, it was natural for me to grow a fund interest.

I was excited to spend time with Darren and Denise tonight, and I don't know how I could have survived New York without them. It is odd when I tell my friends about why Denise decided to move here after we did not get married. But I convinced her to move to New York so that she could launch her clothing line. We agreed that no matter what we both would always be in each others life, and I guess you could say we kept our word. Darren already wanted to move here with me, so convincing him was not even an issue. I got off at my exit and then I headed straight to Gayle's. When I drove by the restaurant I could see that there were no parking spaces, so I decided to park a few blocks away. I found a parking space, and then checked the parking meter before walking the few blocks to the restaurant. I crossed the street and approached the entrance of Gayle's, and I spotted Denise right away. She was wearing a beautiful brown knee length leather coat, and a yellow and orange scarf which I am quite sure was a part of her signature collection. In college, Denise was noted as one of the best looking women on campus. Whenever I would go places with her I would catch most of the men staring at Denise. They seemed almost intoxicated by her looks.

"Hello, looking for someone in particular?" I asked as I stood behind her."

"As a matter of fact, I am. I am supposed to meet this guy here. He's about six feet tall, he has butter pecan colored skin, the thickest eyelashes I have ever seen, a chiseled body, soft curly black hair, and was handsome last time I saw him. Have you seen him around?" Denise asked with a smirk on her face.

"Well as a matter of fact I have. He's standing right here!" I laughed.

"Oh, I remembered someone much taller. Damn Jay it's just you."

"You're crazy Denise. Let's go in and get a table." I suggested as I opened the door for her.

As we entered Gayle's I could really feel the soul of this joint. The place was dimly lit with small black lamps on each table, and I could hear the soulful sounds of jazz playing the background. Our waiter seated us at our table, and I immediately wanted to know what was up with Denise.

"How was your day?" Denise asked as we sat down.

"Nothing has happened any different than from the last time I talked to you. How was your day?"

"Okay, but it would have been better if I could have gotten Anthony to invest in my clothing line." Denise replied.

"I meant to ask you how that was going."

"Well, I'm supposed to do a fashion show in three months with Shawano Fuqua. She came by my boutique on Fifth Avenue and loved my designs."

"So why do you need Anthony to invest in your clothing line?" I asked.

"He has major connections. I know he can help me become a national signature."

"I'm very proud of you," I replied as I looked at my watch. "Where is Darren?"

"He called and said he would be running a little late. Oh there he is coming in the door," Denise said, as she signaled with her hands in a wave motion so that Darren would know where we were sitting.

Darren and I had been best friends every since we were toddlers. His family and my family were all long time friends. Our mother's are sorority sisters and also best friends. So it was expected that Darren and I would have an instant liking to each other. Darren's father was the president of *Gamma Gamma Phi* when he attended *Terminus University* so Darren was legacy. This meant that he was guaranteed a place in the fraternity. When your mother or father is in the same fraternity or sorority you want to join becoming a member is inevitable I guess you could say. My sister Tonya was a legacy because my mother was in the sister sorority to my fraternity which was called *Gamma Gamma Nu*. I grew a fond interest in *Gamma Gamma Phi* every since Darren and his father insisted that I pledge. My father was not around as much, so Darren's father mentored me as if I were one of the Cunningham men. I stood up to greet Darren, he gave me the secret fraternal hand grip, and then he kissed Denise on the cheek.

"What's up Jay?" Darren asked as he searched the menu.

"Nothing much bro, nothing much. What's been up with you man?"

"I'm beat, man. I'm sure glad that tonight is Friday!" Darren said as he took off his coat.

"I heard that," Denise said. "How's that Baker case you have been working on going Darren?"

"Oh I'm glad it's finally over. Thank God. I finally won today after weeks of being in the courtroom defending my client."

"What are you guys talking about?" I asked with a puzzled expression on my face.

"My client Linda Baker recently sued her hairdresser for taking out her hair."

"The relaxer the stylist put in her hair was not compatible to what she normally used," Denise explained. "That's why I let Belinda style my hair honey. It's not good to switch up on hair dressers unless you know their client base and their experience. Hello somebody." Denise said as if she was testifying in church.

"Well, I won the case," Darren cheerfully announced.

"That's wonderful Darren. Congratulations." Denise exclaimed.

"Let's celebrate. Dinner's on me guys!" Darren insisted.

I did not object, and I was happy for Darren. He's a good lawyer, and I have used him from time to time for different legal matters I had to handle. He also just made senior partner at the firm he has been at for over four years now. I always am very excited to hear of his victories in court each time he shares them with me. The three of us talked for a while over dinner discussing our day at work, and my annual Christmas party, which was coming up soon. We started the lunch and dinner socials back when we were in college. Each one of us grew up eating dinner around the table with our families to discuss our day, so it was natural for us to meet and break bread together. When the three of us do get together we know its going to be at a dining spot. We also know that a last minute lunch appointment means that something serious needs to be said. Ron Deheem performed and his showcase was really sensational. I enjoyed seeing the poets and singers in person rather than to listen to them on a CD, or watch a DVD of their performances. Later on, there was a jazz segment showcasing some of the local new talent. They actually had some good acts, but what stood out to me the most was one of the singers named Donnie. His falsetto and soulful voice kind of reminded me of the R&B sensation Maxwell. Denise and Darren seemed to have enjoyed themselves, so I could see Gayle's as our new meeting spot.

I looked at my watch and realized that it was getting late. Denise looked as if she had too much to drink, so I asked Darren to follow her home and call me when he got to her house. I would have followed her home but I had to get some rest because tomorrow I was going to trade my car in for a new Mercedes G-Wagon. Ever since I was a child, I always dreamed that one-day I would become a successful doctor and own a Mercedes. I must say that I am blessed because only the Lord could have really provided me all the prosperity I enjoy today. Everyday I realize that I could be on the streets, on drugs, or jobless. So every day, every second, and every minute I give God praise for all He has done for me.

When I got home, I kicked off my shoes and fell straight onto the couch. I was almost asleep when I realized that I had to get up and make sure that I was safe and secure before going to bed. I have a tendency of rushing in the house and sometimes I forget to lock the front door. I really needed to be more careful after Ms. Clara told me that she saw a mysterious person stop by my front door today. Just thinking about someone being in my house uninvited while I was asleep sent chills all over my body. I locked the front door and then I set all three of my alarm clocks. I have one on the desk in my home office across from my bedroom, one on the television, and a reliable alarm clock next to my bed. I have never been a person who could just wake up and start my day like a normal person. With me, I have to roll over, look at the clock two or three times, and then sit upward at the edge of the bed. This ritual has been consistent ever since I was a little boy. I remember my mother used to come upstairs and get on my last nerve with her good morning greetings. It never failed; every morning before school there she was, at the foot of the bed singing.

Sundays were the worst because we had to get up at the crack of dawn. I was a minister's son and so that meant we were exclusively involved in church. I was at Sunday school, and even first, second, and sometimes third service if my mother felt the strength to go. Which unfortunately the woman did, I will say she really loved her Lord and Savior. And oh my God please don't let my mother or the Pastor have to preach somewhere. My sister and I would find ourselves involuntarily drawn to every venue she went to. I have not been to church in a while, but could you blame me? I mean I was in church mostly all of my life. I love God don't get me wrong but I think taking a few Sundays off is not committing a sin. Besides, I have enough bible verses in my head to save me for a lifetime.

As I was turning my cell phone on silent ring I suddenly remembered that I had gotten a package earlier today. I left the package in the trunk of my car. I guess you could say I did not see an urgency to open it anytime soon. Sleep finally made its way to my brain as I tried to nestle in the comfort of the blanket on my sofa. I always kept a blanket on the sofa in my bedroom because I spend a lot of nights sleeping on the sofa than in my bed. The painful thought of sleeping in my bed alone was something I did not want to get used to feeling. However, for the past ten years of my life I have grown to just deal with it. "Damn! It would be nice to hold someone tonight instead of these pillows," I protested as if someone other than me was listening. I turned the lamp off over the night stand, and I gave the pillows a tight squeeze. As I stared at the alarm clock on the dresser across the room it seemed as though the morning would not come fast enough.

Chapter 2

THIS MORNING, I WOKE UP earlier than usual so that I could get an early start of the day. Before my feet touched the floor, I took a moment of silence to give reverence to the Lord for His grace and His mercy. I realized what a blessing it was to simply wake up one more day. No matter the source of my haste, I had to start my days by thanking God. It was my way of keeping humble and to keep myself against any perils that might lie ahead of me. I stumbled to the entertainment room and pulled the drapes away from the window. The sunshine welcomed me with its intense light and optimism for a great day ahead. "Hmm," I thought as a warm nostalgic feeling entered with the sunlight. Two words were apparent as I took advantage of waking up alone and that was a country breakfast. I decided that I would cook myself a home cooked meal so I headed to the kitchen. As the grits slowly bubbled on the back burner, and the country fried steak made its own gravy, I thought of my sister Tonya. She was the one that taught me how to cook when we were younger. She always wanted to own her own catering business, but instead she settled on getting a degree in Business Administration. Cooking remained her passion as she continued to hone her skills on my mother and the rest of our family.

The extra time I spent in the kitchen left me in a bit of a time crunch and I began my usual routine of racing to the beat of the second hand on the clock as I prepared myself to leave for New Jersey. As I was turning the stove off, my syncopated pace was broken by the sound of the telephone, which had a way of annoying me whenever I was on one of my hurried excursions through my condo. It was no surprise to me that the call was from Tonya. I let her anxiousness drown my annoyed tone as I picked up on her apparent anxiety.

"Were you asleep?" She asked as if it mattered. She would have continued anyway even if my answer had been yes.

"No I'm up and I was trying to get ready to get out of here and eat a little bit of breakfast. That is before the phone rang." I shot back in a playful sarcastic tone. Before I could ask her what was wrong she barreled right through the conversation, which did not leave any room for a comment from me.

As to be expected, Tonya was anxious about her up coming nuptials to Brian. Her verbal baggage included having boots with my mother over flowers, colors for the wedding, and some other nonsense, which I had little interest in. Of course it didn't matter if I had because she never let me get a word in. So I continued to fix myself some breakfast as I tried to get a few bites in before I left.

"You know I swear sometimes she can really go overboard," she sighed as she finally ran out of breath or complaints. It was hard to tell what was really going on. My brotherly instinct finally had an opportunity to come out as I assured her that she would endure my mother's madness and that marrying Brian was the right choice.

"You're right," she concluded. "I do have her under control. I remind her all the time that it's my wedding not hers," she said trying to convince me when we both knew the real truth. We broke the three seconds of silence with a laugh, and I began my descent off the phone. She picked up on what I thought was a subtle hint to get her off the phone.

"Now where are you going Jackson in such a hurry so early on a Saturday morning?" She demanded. If anyone knew of my obsession with time it was Tonya.

"Out to Newark. I pick up the car today! I've got to get going to beat traffic," I rushed back at her.

"Jackson it's Saturday! You might as well calm down because there is hardly any traffic anywhere on Saturday mornings." Tonya never lived in New York or New Jersey so her comment about the way traffic operated here humored me.

"Tonya you will see when you come to visit me that it is very busy on the weekends. Look, I have to go so I will have to catch up with you later. Give mother a kiss for me and tell her I love her."

"I will Jackson, talk to you later." She said as we ended the call.

I finished getting dressed and I was ready to leave when I remembered the package I left in my car. I am not sure why I keep making excuses on not reviewing it but I will get around to it. Perhaps there was just something sinister about the package that made me nervous. The drive over to Newark was exciting because I had to cross the *George Washington Bridge* to get to the dealership. It amazes me that this bridge has been around since 1931, and it still is standing today as a world landmark. I have always had a great appreciation for many of the world's landmarks and historical sites. However, this bridge stood out the most to me because it told so many stories without ever being heard by the human ear. Millions of Americans have traveled back and forth on this bridge, and to me that is astonishing because of its pillar of strength and gateways to various destinations. An hour later I finally reached the dealership and for a minute I became very sentimental about the trade. I have had this car for a few years but my lease was up. It seems as though this trade has brought back so many memories of the first day I got it and what I was going through at that time in my life. But the car did need a few repairs, and I am always a person who has to have the latest gadgets, clothes, and the latest car model, so it was expected of me to want something new. As I pulled up I could see the salesman walking out the double glass doors. I got out of my car and greeted him with a smile. He was a very husky Hispanic guy with short slick black hair. Darren referred me to him when I was first looking for a car.

"Hello Dr. Phillips," he said. "It's so good to see you again my friend."

"Good to see you as well Jose," I said as I shook his massive right hand.

"We just got a few of these models right after you called last week," he said, as he walked me through the lot. "This is our new 2009 Mercedes G-Wagon model. We have three colors to choose from."

"I like the silver one," I said.

"Great choice Dr. Phillips! I'm glad to be doing business with you again. Let's go inside and fill out the papers."

"I can't wait to drive this baby home," I cheered.

After thirty minutes, Jose was really getting on my nerves with all the paperwork I had to fill out. Jose said that the trade would take a few more minutes. That's because he had to do a few things, and then I would be able to take my new car home. My cell phone had been on silent ring while I was in the office, so I didn't know until I looked at my phone that I had missed any calls. I excused myself and went outside to check my voice mail. To my surprise I had an urgent message and then two more messages. Thinking it was either my mother or Denise, I skipped over the other messages. The urgent message was from someone who said that they wanted to know if I had received their package yet. They asked me to give them a call whenever I got the message. This person sounded familiar, but for some reason I couldn't place it.

"The car is all yours Dr. Phillips," Jose said interrupting my thoughts.

"Wonderful! Thanks very much," I replied cheerfully.

"You also left this box in the backseat. It looked important so I thought you might have forgotten it."

"Oh yeah it kind of is. Thank you," I said as I stared at the box.

"Great doing business with you Dr. Phillips," he said as he shook my right hand. "Come and see us anytime."

"You know I will," I replied as I twirled the key ring with my new car keys around my index finger.

After I got inside the car I spent ten minutes looking at all the features. It had a navigational system with full maps and a touch-screen control on the 6 CD stereo system. This model had all of the amenities I needed to keep me well pleased and entertained when I did drive. I suddenly snapped out of my trance and remembered I had to see what the message on my voice mailbox was all about. I started the engine, exhaled, fastened my seat belt, and immediately rushed home. For some odd reason my heart started to thump harder as the anticipation of what this was all about began to make me feel uneasy. Even though

I did not know what was going on, something within me predicted it would not be good. So I slowed down and took my time getting home. The package was on the left seat in my car and in between red lights I would look at it. One hour later I finally pulled up to my home and then I took the box with me upstairs. When I got inside my condo I sat down on my bed and then began opening the box. There was a Waterford crystal wine decanter inside with two highball crystal glasses. As my hands sifted through the Styrofoam packaging peanuts I stumbled upon a note at the bottom of the box, and a letter typed on granite colored paper attached to a paste colored index sized card. I gazed for a while at the crystal gift and smiled at the thought that someone would send me something so expensive and elegant. I never paid much attention to the senders address because all I was focused on was the urgent yellow florescent colored sticker on the box. To my surprise the sender did not include their address on the box. Thinking it was probably from Yolanda or Eric I placed the gift on the end table on the side of my bed, and sat down on my sofa to read the letter.

Hey Jackson, This is J.B. writing you to express the way I have always felt about you. I always wanted to go further with our relationship in college, but I never had the courage to tell you face to face. Please don't be mad at me. I hope that you understand that I was on the basketball team and in other political positions on campus, and I had a reputation to protect. But I always thought about you when we would pass each other on campus. I always knew you still had feelings for me after we were together a few times.

I can't change the past, but all I can say is that I'm here now. As selfish as it may sound about shielding my reputation, I had to. I'm sorry and I hope you understand. I'll call back later this week when I think you have read this letter. I went to great lengths to track you down. I am not going to reveal the source that gave me all of your information. But after we talk and you decide that you do or don't see a future for us, I will either leave you alone or try and make us work.

Give it some thought...J. B.

After the shock of the letter began to fade, I found myself gazing out of my bedroom window. The view of the park nearby always had a soothing effect on me when I felt stressed out of sorts. It's so hard to believe that after all these years there remained some unfinished business between J.B. and I. Somehow the years between graduation and now allowed my memory to fade as I began to recall that J.B. was originally from New York. So today's surprise really isn't so surprising after all. "J.B." landed at *Terminus* after being heavily recruited from high school. A stellar college basketball career, not to mention being the captain of the team, paved the way to a career playing pro-ball. A parent's urging to launch a "fall-back" plan paved the way to law school, as it would seem a career in law had more longevity than any short lived career in the spotlight. Procrastinating no longer, I finally mustered up enough nerves to dial the number left on my voice mail. I exhaled my brief relief when the answering machine began to recite its recorded message.

The sudden turn of events drained what remained of my energy and let my futile attempt to reach "J.B." lead me to give up on reaching him. The need to pray seemed to be helpful but I found myself questioning whether God was some how angry with me. I mean, I thought I left these feelings for J.B. back in undergrad. The gift and more so the letter ignited the emotions that sat repressed inside of me and now held me in a ball of confusion. I tried to pray for God to give me direction on how to deal with all of this, but concentrating was nearly impossible. I sat the whole evening watching reruns on television as I drunk continuously from the bottle of wine I picked up yesterday. The wine acted as my aide of companionship as I tried to erase any memory of J. B. and the lie I have been living mostly all of my adult life. I turned my phone off and I drunk some more and some more to try and erase the hurt, shame, and guilt I was feeling. I had spent hours glued in one place on my bedroom floor and I later realized that it was now midnight. For over nine hours I had been sitting in my room beating myself up for having to deal with any of this.

To talk about my past is something that I thought I would never have to do. This is why I became a counselor, so I could counsel others, and at the same time find healing vicariously through each one of them. I got the strength to pull myself up off the floor and into my bathroom. The wine and the pain made my body hot all over and so I ran some cold water in the sink on a face towel so I could cool down. As I stared at myself in the mirror I began to cry again as I came to grips that I was a lie. My whole life has been nothing more then a big fat lie. But I have to pull it together. I have to show no signs of defeat. This is something that I master very well, but with the letter and the gift perhaps this time I will not be able to do that. I washed my face and then brushed my teeth before heading to bed, and then I stripped myself down until I did not have on anymore clothes.

Metaphorically I saw my nakedness as wholeness, being stripped of all I ever was is what I truly needed to get me through all of this. Tonight I found my body leading me to my bed, a place I never really slept in. But tonight I wanted to feel small in such a big space, hoping that my large king sized bed could be a sole heir of protection to me. "The Devil is always on his job," I whispered as I my body became paralyzed in my own thoughts. A fear found its way to my pillow as I tried to lull myself.

Chapter 3

I SLEPT THE WHOLE DAY Sunday, and lounged around on Monday completing a few tasks here and there. One of the early signs of depression is to miss meals and sleep a lot. Here lately that has been the case with me because I felt that if I stayed awake I would have to deal with my reality. I arrived at my office at twelve thirty because I had a session with Mr. and Mrs. Sanders. They were my only clients for the day, and after their session I could get back into bed. I would have gotten to the office a little earlier but I had to push myself to get up. After I received the letter I became distraught and I resulted to drinking heavily. My mind took a roller coaster spin as the past I had left alone for some many years came back to confront me full circle. I collected my scattered thoughts and then I sat at my desk awaiting my twelve thirty appointment. The clock read twelve forty which meant they were running ten minutes late. Moments later Sheila entered my office and told me that Mr. And Mrs. Sander had arrived. I took out my pen and yellow note pad and then I instructed Sheila to let them in.

"Hi Mrs. Sanders. How are you doing today?" I asked as they both sat down.

"I'm just fine, Dr. Phillips," Mrs. Sanders replied as she looked at her husband.

"What about you Mr. Sanders. How are you doing today sir?" I asked.

"I guess my day has been okay, until I came here, Dr. Phillips," Mr. Sanders replied.

"Let me get out your file," I said as I went to my file cabinet. I hoped they would have made some more progress since their last session. They had argued back and forth, and Mrs. Sanders had threatened to slap him.

"Okay, let's get started," I continued. "Last session, we discussed the possibility of you two taking time to go on a cruise. Are you ready for something like that?"

"Yeah, I suppose George and I could use a little vacation. This would probably give us a chance to talk things over," Mrs. Sanders replied.

"This will also help you rekindle the love you once had for each other. Communication is a key factor here for the both of you. Think of this as another honeymoon. But before you two do that, Patricia I want you to look at George and tell him how you really feel. Tell him what you have been holding inside."

"Well George, I just feel for the past two months now you don't have time for me anymore. I mean yes, I am glad that business is picking up for you, but what about me? I am so sick and tired of waiting for you night after night. I feel alone George. You hear me? Alone!" She screamed.

"George what is your response to how Patricia is feeling right now?"

"Patricia right now the company is my main focus. It's not that I don't love you, but I'm trying to make a better future for the both of us." George pleaded.

"Both of us? You mean us and me, or us as in you and what's her damn name? Just what is her name George?" Patricia shot back unexpectedly. George sat up at attention nervously trying to find his voice. Unfortunately all he could come up with was a nervous stammer of a man who was just busted by his wife. Patricia left little room for an answer that did not include the nervous babble of expected denial.

I must say, in my most professional analysis I never saw that coming.

Fighting the urge to nervously stammer myself, I had to pretend that this was normal and jump right in to mediate.

"George I think Patricia deserves an answer. Are you currently having and affair?"

"It's not what she thinks I met her at local bar named Smith's, this bar in Harlem. I needed a drink to escape the pressures of my business and my wife's constant nagging. We talked about nothing important at first, and then more about some of the challenges at the job, home life, you know the usual. And what was so funny is that here she was a total stranger, and I talked to her as if I had known her forever. And what's more funny is she seemed to listen to me. She just listened and seemed to be very interested in anything and everything that I had to say to her. I felt at ease with her and I thought that was strange, and usually I'm not that way, especially around people I don't know."

George paused for a moment as Mrs. Sanders sat still and listened without jumping in. Her eyes glistened while she tried to refrain from crying.

"Well, before we left, we exchanged numbers," he continued. "Of course I explained that I was married and she said that was obvious to her when she approached me. Well, when I got outside its like reality hit me in the face like a burst of cold air. I then asked myself, what am I doing? I can't do this! I love my wife. There was a trash can on the corner on the way to the car. I took the paper with her number on it and threw it away. I thought that it would be over being that I thought she would have wanted me to call her first. But to my surprise she called me first and said she wanted to see me. That is when I agreed to at least have lunch with her. And again the same thing happened when we had lunch we laughed and talked. But when I left her to go back to my office I began to feel a little guilty for having lunch with her."

He broke his trance briefly as he looked at his wife. Her silence held steadfast but her tears had broken through and began the descent down her face.

"I promise you nothing happened honey. Nothing happened. We just met for lunch from time to time, and some times we met after work and had a drink. But it was just talking that is all." He paused again and intensified his gaze directly into her eyes. He drew in a deep breath before he continued and I began to brace myself for the worst.

"But honey, I have to tell you because this has been tearing me up. The guilt, I just can't stand the guilt. I mean after all, that's why we're here now. Is that why we are? Somebody tell me!" He looked to me desperate for affirmation. I gave him the nod to continue.

"I..., well there was this one time we did meet up. This time it was not for lunch or a drink, this time we met at her house. The bar was crowded and I couldn't hear her talking. So she invited me to her place so we could talk in private she said. I hesitated at first, but then I thought it was just talking and nothing else would happen. But I was wrong things did get a little heated and before I knew it I ended up kissing her. But I couldn't go any further. I know you may not believe what I am saying but I swear that is all that happened. All we did is talked I swear of it. Now is that cheating?"

George's inquiry was more than just rhetoric. He honestly had not seen the harm in what happened between the both of them. I explained to Mr. Sanders the concept of emotional cheating and how it compares to physical cheating. His ease and comfort with Cindy was probably the same comfort he felt when he first met his wife. Mr. Sanders sat up, cleared his throat, and finally broke his wife's silence.

"I feel betrayed because my husband can talk to me. I am his wife, so if there is something wrong he needs to talk to me, not this home wrecker. I love you George. I just want the man I married back. I only say I am busy because I am mad at you for not giving me the quality time I need and so rightfully deserve. I want our marriage to work. We have children! Remember them George? Jonathon is always crying because he wants his daddy to be at his basketball games. And then there is Mariah; you know how she loves you so much. She asked me the other day if we were getting a divorce. Think about your family!"

Mrs. Sanders let loose and began to sob openly. Yet she leaned towards George who in turn comforted her hands against his shoulder. Their marriage was far from over, yet a little lost.

"What I am hearing from the both of you is that you need to communicate better with each other. Communication is a key factor here as I said before. I still think going on this trip would be a very great thing to do. This way you can see if you can make this marriage work. I think you can do it, but George you have to tell Cindy that you cannot see or talk to her anymore. Having a relationship the way you two do is not the solution to saving your marriage. The children don't need to see you both argue. Put yourselves in their shoes. And George you should not create more problems by not being at any of Jonathon's games. Both parents should help raise these children not one."

"I'm giving you two a homework assignment to start doing tonight. After the kids are settled in I want you both to have a nice dinner. Pull out the registry China that you never use, light a few candles, and put on some soft music. Don't try and focus on work, the kids, or what is wrong in your marriage. I want you two to just absorb the stillness and peace of having some alone time together for a change. Then do the dishes together, wipe the table down, and sit on the sofa and watch your favorite movie or television show. Before going to bed tonight you both get a piece of paper and a pen and write down what you like about each other. I want you to do this daily and read it back to each other so you both can see why you are made for each other. Meanwhile I want you two to go on a vacation as I recommended during your last visit. After you have done all of that I want you to come back to my office and let me know of your progress. Now will you do it?" I asked expecting some opposition especially from Mr. Sanders.

"Well I don't know Dr. Phillips. I mean that trip sounds nice and all but I am not sure I can be gone long. I mean how long will I have to stay away from my business?" George asked as he started his predictable objections. But Mrs. Sanders stopped him dead in his tracks before I could answer him.

"Yeah, uh whatever! Your business, our business will be just fine George. We will do this! Down to every detail that Dr. Phillips has instructed us to do." Mrs. Sanders demanded without approval from Mr. Sanders.

"Great! I think you both get the idea." I assured them.

"Oh we get it. We get it huh George?" Mrs. Sanders retorted. Her line of questioning was very much rhetorical.

"Sure, I get it Dr. Phillips. Thanks for your support thus far Dr. Phillips." George replied humbly. We shook hands as gentlemen and I gave Mrs. Sanders a hug of reassurance. They rushed through the office door with the enthusiasm of newly weds. Sheila paused from her computer and stared in disbelief.

"What's gotten into those two? Usually they come in here dragging and leave out yelling. What did you say to them? She asked with her gaze still fixed on the door.

"Can't tell you. Its patient and doctor confidentiality." I bragged.

"Oh yeah! I forgot," Sheila replied still in disbelief.

I gathered all of my belongings and decided that I would give Darren a call to see if he and Denise wanted to stop by my place tonight after church. The three of us have not hung out at my house in a while and I didn't want to be alone when I went home. I was still shook up from the letter. I needed to be around my friends to uplift my spirits. I called Darren to see if he wanted to join me for lunch today being that I had no more plans until later tonight to go to Tuesday night service.

"Hey Darren," I said after he answered the phone.

"What's up man?" Darren replied.

"What are you doing today?" I asked.

"Nothing but trying to finish these papers up on this Coca case I told you I was working on. That's all. Why? What's up bro?"

"Oh I just wanted to know if you wanted to go out to lunch with me. That's all."

"Oh sure that's cool. I'm getting hungry. Let's go to that place called Barry's on 135th street corner of Lenox."

"That sounds great. I'll meet you in a few man. Does that sound good?"

"Yeah bro'. That's cool."

On my way to meet Darren for lunch I thought about if it was a good idea to tell him about my plight. I didn't know how he would react to my confession, and so I suddenly became afraid. Traffic was not that bad for the midday lunch rush, and I was able to find a parking space as well. Barry's was very popular for lunch goers, and Sheila and I would come here often to have lunch. When I got inside of the restaurant I did not see a trace of Darren anywhere. So, I decided that I would just go inside and order my food while I waited on him. I found a table for two over near the entrance of the restaurant so he could spot me easily.

"Welcome to Barry's, sir. What will you have today?" The waitress asked as she pulled a black pen out of her hair.

"I would like two chicken platters, one with baked potato and black beans, and the other one with black beans and rice."

"Eating for two?" She jibed as she reached over the table to remove the menus.

"No, no and I don't have an imaginary friend." I laughed. "I'm meeting my brother. He should be on his way in a few minutes," I continued as I looked towards the door for Darren in frantic anticipation.

"Oh, I get it," She smiled back. "I'll bring his order after he arrives. What will the two of you want to drink?" She asked pointing to the empty seat across from me. She retained her grin as though we shared a secret inside joke.

"Cola's, one with ice, and one without ice." I answered quickly anxiously waiting for the awkwardness to pass.

"You and your brother must be really close, you two even eat the same," She quipped. "I will be back with your drinks," she said as she disappeared to the kitchen.

She was partially right. Darren and I were close even though we were not officially related. Still we had been through so much together through the years. Our bond was a brotherhood of sorts being that our habits had rubbed off on each other.

I looked at my watch and I wondered what was keeping Darren. While I was searching my phone to dial him, I looked up and saw him coming towards me. I could also see that he brought his work with him. He was carrying two manila office folders in his right hand.

"I'm running a little late because I had to wrap something up real quick at the office. Where is our waitress?" He asked as he loosened his tie.

I laughed to myself because she was headed towards the table with our drinks. As she placed them in front of us Darren looked puzzled as she placed the Cola with extra ice right in front of him. Darren's mouth dropped open in disbelief. Then I told him I had already ordered for us.

"Good! You know what I like. Besides I don't have that much time. I have to get back to the office."

"Oh I understand. But overall how has your day been?" I asked.

"It's been fair for the most part. I also have to finish showing the auditor around the office."

"Oh an audit. Is it that time of year already?" I asked.

"Yeah this guy is an auditor, and he just moved back to New York from Atlanta. He went to school there and started working after he graduated."

"You seem to know a lot about this guy. Is he someone you know?"

"Well as a matter of fact I do man. Guess where he went to school?"

"Um, Bethune-Cookman, " I blurted out. Darren rolled his eyes as if to say, "you big dummy."

"No man! It turns out he's Jamal Brown. He played basketball for Terminus University while we were there."

I tried to look nonchalant as I pretended to search my memory. I took a drink from my glass and my sip turned into a full fledge choke. The truth of the matter was that the news shocked me. I tried to recover quickly but my Cola just wouldn't go down the right way.

"You okay man?" Darren asked as he attempted to pat me on the back.

I rejected his assistance with a quick draw of my hand as I reached for my napkin and I turned my head away.

"I am fine Darren. It just went down the wrong way." I lied. The truth is that the news hit me like a ton of bricks, and the impact was enough to send me under the table. I prayed that Darren would not sense my sudden uneasiness.

"It's a small world Darren. Out of all the auditors in New York you get one that graduated from T.U." I managed to recover hopefully distracting Darren's attention away from me.

"Imagine that! I remember him from playing basketball but we were not friends. How about you, do you know him man?"

"No I can't say I did. You know I'm not that much into basketball. I mean, besides, how would I know him? I mean he wasn't in our frat or nothing. Why would I even be associated with him?" My nerves began to take over as I wrestled with blurting out the truth with continuing the charade.

"Chill man. I just thought you might have remembered him that's all."Darren defended. Darren's look made me squirm even more. It was times like these that I hated that he and I were so close. I took another sip, this time long and deliberate. I needed a few seconds to recover.

"Well come to think of it I do remember a Jamal in my dorm.

I think he lived on the same floor as I did." I threw Darren a bone. Hopefully it would be enough to move the conversation along. I kept pleading in my mind for him to change the subject.

The waitress finally pays us a visit with our food. I've been redeemed. A chance finally to change the damn subject.

"Sorry about the wait gentlemen." The waitress interjected. She placed the food on the table and turned to leave. That is when Darren had to put a final thought on the subject.

"Like I said it's a small world by having him be my auditor. Maybe a blessing though. I don't think he will find anything wrong because my files are impeccable. But you know it can't hurt to have an alum on your side."

"You are right that does help." I replied. A few seconds rolled by but at a snails pace while we both stuffed our faces in our plates. Darren pulls his face up and successfully finds something else to talk about. That's when I let out a sigh of relief.

"So, how's your mom doing?" Darren asked. As we started to eat, he finally changed the topic of discussion.

"She should be doing just fine. But she is driving my sister Tonya crazy these days. Tonya is getting married soon and my mother is really getting on my sister's nerves. I have to call her later anyways to get her version of the story because I already talked to my sister Tonya about it."

"Well tell her I said hello when you do speak to her. I haven't seen her in a long time."

"Sure Darren."

Suddenly Darren dropped his fork back to his plate as he looked at his watch. He began to hurriedly scoop one more fork full in his mouth.

"Oh shoot! I have to get back to the office," he shouted as he wiped the last crumbs from his mouth.

"But you just got here. What is the rush?" I asked, looking puzzled.

"I forgot I have to be in court at two thirty today. So that means I have to get my files together before the trial. This case has been taking a lot of my time."

"Okay man. Good luck in court." I said.

"Thanks bro', I will see you and Denise later on in church tonight."

And poof, just like that he was gone. I stayed long enough to finish my wings and pay the check for the both of us. When I reached my car it dawned on me that I was suddenly left with no plans for the rest of the afternoon. Therefore, I headed home in no particular hurry. My energy remained at peak levels as I found myself suddenly available to do some things I usually put off because of constantly having to rush out somewhere. Several possibilities presented themselves as I meandered through each task. One of my favorite movies was on, *Love Jones,* and I let it play in the background occasionally tuning in on the good parts. A trip to my closet to find clothes to wear to Tuesday night service suddenly pitted me in the battle of the bulge as I finally stood face to face with the stressful task of organizing my closet. The massive walk-ins were the one amenity that forced me to sign the dotted line when I first viewed this place. What I once believed was a God send for my wardrobe, was now the hassle of my existence. The task left me drained, yet satisfied in that I now had a strong sense of accomplishment. My mind played back other loose ends I needed to tie up since I finally had some time on my hands. So I decided to check in with my mother since it had been a few days since we last spoke to each other.

"Hello. Phillips residence," my mother answered in her usual formal fashion.

"Hey, how you doing Ma?"

"I'm just fine baby, but where have you been? I have been calling you for days now. You had me worried, son."

"Sorry Ma. I've been extremely busy all week. But I wasn't too busy to call you Ma, I know."

"How's life in New York and the world of offices?"

"Everything is fine here, and business is still going well."

"I know... You really love your work. I hear it every time we talk son."

"Yes I do Ma. As long as I have clients, I have a job." I joked.

"You're so crazy Jay. Just don't get so busy where you can't make your sister's wedding."

"I have already cleared my schedule so don't worry about that."

"My daughter is getting married. I still can't believe it."

"She called me the other day and was a little nervous. But I know that she is very excited."

"Yes she is. Everyday we are looking for things for her and her new husband's house. My energy is gone. That girl wants to go here and there. I don't think my feet can take all that walking anymore."

"Well does she need anything else, Ma?"

"No, just her big brother walking her down the aisle, that's all."

"What do you want me to do about a tuxedo?" I asked.

"I have already taken care of that by setting you up for an appointment to get fitted son. You just make sure you get here."

"Yes Ma."

"Are you going to church tonight?"

"Yes, I'm going with Denise and Darren."

"Wonderful! Tell the both of them I said hello."

"Oh I will. Darren has been asking me about you, so I'll tell him you said hello. I love you Ma."

"I love you too baby."

"Well I'll call soon. Kiss Tonya for me."

"I will make sure that I do that. Bye son."

"Love you, Ma."

As soon as I hung up the phone with my mother, I took a shower, and then popped some popcorn so that I could watch the rest of the movie. *Love Jones* is a romantic story about two people who are madly in love with each other. Throughout their relationship, they face a lot of obstacles in their relationship before they both realize how much they really do love each other. The plot kind of reminded me of the relationship I once had with Denise. As I sat on the couch, I wondered if I ever would find true love like the characters in the movie. Tears streamed down my face. And the agony of growing old and alone made my heart ache another day. After the movie went off I spent the rest of the afternoon sorting though bills, unread letters, and I even decided to fold a few clothes and store them away. Whitney Houston's voice could be heard throughout my condo as I traveled from room to room cleaning and trying to keep myself busy. I felt that if I could stay busy then I could keep my mind off of the issues. I danced to all of Whitney's greatest hits, and some songs made me happy, some songs made me sad, but I was grateful that her music could comfort me.

Church started at seven o' clock tonight and there was a determination inside of me that would not let anything stop me from going. I knew that going to church was a real big step for me to take. But God is the only one that I feel I can turn to in times like these. I hadn't heard from J.B. since receiving the package. I also couldn't figure out how he was able to contact me. My phone number was after all unlisted. The only way he found me is probably through Darren. But I didn't know why Darren would give him my address and phone number and not inform me. I have let a lot of things I have done in my past go unresolved for so long until now it has resurfaced. I was raised to give all of my problems to God, but I assumed that He already knew what I have been dealing with. Therefore, I did not see the need to confess to Him about all of my issues. I sometimes wished that I would bring my problems to God more often, and then perhaps I would not be in the mess I am in now.

I left the house at about six o' clock and I felt a cloud of peace reign over me. I had been waiting for this type of emotion, but I did not know when it would come my way. I wanted to be happy, to be whole, to be free, and to be heard. It's funny because we all hide behind masks at some point in our lives. Some maybe longer than others, but most of us do show other's our representatives and not who we really are. I just want to end all of my depression and denial tonight. I have always been so secretive, and I have never wanted anyone to know anything about my personal affairs. However, there comes a time in life when you have to be true to your self and stop the masquerading.

As I approached the church I began the process of hiding my depressed mood. If I did not show any defeated symptoms then no one would ask me, "Jackson are you okay?" Darren and Denise knew me too well so I was not always good at hiding a lot from them. When I entered the cathedral, I spotted Denise standing up clapping her hands. Darren saw me and motioned for me to come over to where they both were sitting. Pastor Clark took the podium as we all followed his instructions to greet our neighbor. Then Pastor Clark went into his formal greeting and informed us of his topic for the night.

"Good evening and welcome to the house of the Lord," he began. "Tonight I will be reading from Psalms 1, and then I will go into my message, *'Give it to Jesus.'*"

As the minister preached, I asked God to show me a sign that He would help me get through this storm. No one knew it but I was torn up inside, and if God didn't help me I was so sure I would lose control. I really felt the move of the service and at times I caught myself fighting back tears. Church was a place where I found refuge and inspiration. No matter what I had going on during the week I needed to make sure that church was somewhere in my schedule. When I came to church I was not like other church people who cared what other people thought about them. I came to church with no agenda but only to hear a word from God and listen to the mass choir. The problem today is that most people go to church and feel like God does not love them. But God so loved this world until He gave us a second chance in life. If I could not find peace and love in the church then there surely is nowhere else I could find it. The preacher finally finished his sermon after about thirty minutes, and he then asked those in need of prayer to come up to the altar. As I approached the minister he told me that he had heard God speaking to him. The firmness of his grip startled me as I felt some sort of force of energy pull me all over my body. He never broke his gaze as he was speaking, and I felt like it was just me and him only at the service.

"Even though you are struggling right now, know that He is standing nigh," he began with his eyes closed and his head bowed. "God hears you," he assured me.

I wept uncontrollably, and I felt Denise's arms around me. I heard her whisper as she guided me back to my seat that she was here for me.

"Is everything okay Jay?" Darren asked as I sat down.

"Yeah I just caught the spirit," I lied.

For some reason I would not let Denise's hand go. I needed her energy, her touch, and her understanding. Darren still had a strange look on his face, and I even noticed Denise shaking her head as I held on tighter. Surely they both knew something was going on with me. I just hoped that neither one of them would ask me what I was dealing with. I gathered my car keys and followed Denise and Darren out of the church to head to my car. Darren's face still painted a confused expression as he tried to gather why I was so emotionally distraught. Denise held on to my right hand tightly as she tried to assure me that

I was going to be just fine. I let her hand go and then gave her a tight hug as she testified to Darren and I about tonight's service.

"Pastor really preached tonight," Denise exclaimed.

"Lord he did!" Darren agreed. "I definitely needed to hear that message tonight. It really helped me put all of my problems into perspective."

"I am glad you got your breakthrough tonight," Denise said. "God really moved in a powerful way tonight for you Jay. I can see it all over you. But there is more to it than just one getting moved by the service."

"Thank you. I've got to go." I hurriedly replied.

"Get home safe Jay. I'll call you tomorrow." Denise said.

I thought about what Pastor Clark said to me and Denise's last comments before I drove off. Was God really speaking to me? Was I going to get through this storm in my life? Sometimes I felt that Denise knew my secret but I wondered why she never confronted me about it. I was always masculine and hid my secret identity well. However, I felt she always knew deep down inside the truth. Through everything, she always extended her support. Between Denise and Pastor Clark, I felt more secure. He was there giving me the divine word from God, and she was there, as my companion coming to my rescue just as she always does.

I settled into bed and began my nightly ritual of channel surfing. I stumbled upon a Christmas special that caught my attention. The program featured the likes of Aretha Franklin and Whitney Houston putting their spin on the old standards like *"Joy to the World"*, and *"Oh Holy Night."* The show placed me in a festive mood, which was a welcomed change from the moods of despair I had been feeling. My annual holiday party would be more than stellar if I had people like Aretha or Patti there. I watched the rest of the show and then I turned the television off and stared endlessly at the ceiling. I closed my eyes while I let exhaustion take over my body. Sleep finally took over allowing me to escape from the present another night.

Chapter 4

I ARRIVED AT MY OFFICE the next afternoon in typical fashion with my secretary giving me the run down of my schedule. I had been working with a little girl named Jacquelyn, who had been referred to me by Social Services. Sexually molested by her uncle, Jacquelyn displayed suicidal tendencies. I took her case, because unfortunately I had been through a similar experience. It's an experience that can really scar you for life. A suspicion deep down inside often made me speculate that my inner conflict and constant torment was the result of youthful innocence being stripped away in such a cruel way. This was the reason Jacquelyn was a very special case to me. It hurt me to see a little girl suffering the way she was. I hope that I can help her to overcome all of her trauma. But the fact of the matter is she may never totally heal from any of this. She has to one day look her horror in its face and choose dominion over the experience that continues to taunt her. She was scheduled to see me at three o'clock today because she has school. Her mother thought her sessions would be better when she was not in school. I believe she is right about that. Having Jacquelyn go to school after she has had an hour of confessionals with me could make her become a problem in school. As

I continued to prepare for Jacquelyn's session, my secretary interrupted briefly with a call from Mrs. Matthews, Jacquelyn's mother.

"Mrs. Matthews," I answered in surprise knowing she and Jacquelyn were probably in route to the office.

"Hello, Dr. Phillips I'm so sorry to call you with such late notice." She apologized. "We are going to have to reschedule Jacquelyn's session. I didn't realize until yesterday evening that she has a dentist appointment scheduled for today, and she has to keep it. It was so hard to get her in. Could we reschedule for another day?"

"That shouldn't be a problem, Mrs. Matthews although I need to stress to you how important these sessions are to Jacquelyn's recovery," I stressed with great concern.

"I understand completely, Dr. Phillips. Believe me I know how important this is. Since coming to you, I have seen some changes in Jacquelyn's behavior. She seems to be opening up to me a little."

Mrs. Matthews has played an integral role in her daughter's recovery and has committed herself to finding and supporting help for her as well.

"I'll put you through to Shelia and she can set up that next appointment for you. Just make sure Jacquelyn's schedule is clear for me," I offered jokingly.

"You need to not worry sir. She will be there. We both will be there." She reassured me.

"Very well then Mrs. Matthews. I look forward to seeing the both of you real soon. Tell Jacquelyn I said hello and that I am proud of her."

"I will make sure that I do that Dr. Phillips."

I ended the call, only to be interrupted by a call on my cell phone. "Hello," I answered.

"Hey Jay. This is Darren. What are you doing this afternoon?"

"As it turns out, nothing. Why? What's up?"

"I'm on my way now to pick up J.B., and I thought maybe we could stop by this evening. Get a bite to eat or something?"

"That sounds good," I said, wondering why I agreed. "I'm just leaving the office now. My afternoon session was canceled."

"Great. J.B. and I will stop by after we get him checked into his hotel."

"I mean are you sure you want to come over? I mean I know you have a lot of things to do like show him around the office."

"Man are you okay?"

"Yeah why you ask that?" I asked

"Well you have been acting real weird here lately since I have mentioned Jamal. Is there something you need to tell me?"

"Oh no, I am okay. I really am okay Darren." I lied.

"Alright I will take your word. So Jamal and I will be over later on."

"I'll be home," I said as I hung the phone up.

Jacquelyn was my only client so I had no more clients to see today, which left my schedule clear and free. What the hell was I thinking when I told Darren to come on by? Am I ready for this? What exactly are J.B.'s intentions? So many thoughts raced through my mind as I drove home. I've done pretty well here, starting a new life in New York. But I have to admit the loneliness still prevailed heavily and often shields me from finding true happiness. My career has not been able to replace the emptiness I feel each night when I lay in bed alone. I have done a damn good job repressing my shattered childhood, and my backing out on making Denise my wife. I was doing just fine until now. Until J.B. decided to come back into my life again. But why? And why now?

I rushed in the house not wasting anymore time on useless contemplation. Regardless of any "woulda, shoulda, coulda's," the fact remained that Darren and J.B. were on their way over. Soon I would not only have to face J.B. once again, but I also had to face something I had been blocking out for so long. I decided that my time would be better spent removing that "lived in" look from my condo and get the place ready for company.

I left the letter and the gift on the kitchen counter, but I quickly decided to stash it away in my bedroom. That way Darren would not see it. If Darren saw the letter and the gift then J.B. and I would have a lot of explaining to do. I don't think I was ready for something like that right now. In addition to the letter and the gift from J.B., I still had other things around the house that would make Darren suspicious. But he is my best friend and he has a key to my place, but I don't think he has ever searched through my personal belongings.

Darren would never use the keys to my place unless I was locked out or if I was away and needed him to check on my place. Other than that, he would call or be courteous and allow me to buzz him upstairs. But there are rare cases when he would workout at the gym near my house and then stop by and make his way to my refrigerator. However, the package from J. B was not something I wanted him to stumble upon. The ringing of the buzzer downstairs startled me as I snapped out of my trance. I pressed the open button for Darren and J.B. to enter the building. I had been so busy trying to cover up yet another one of my messes until I completely lost track of time. I was on the tenth floor so I knew it would probably take them a few minutes to make their way to my door.

I ran in the bathroom and gave myself a quick inventory in the mirror to make sure I looked my best. As I was walking out of the bathroom I could hear the knock at my front door. They moved quickly it seemed, and I must have miscalculated how long it would take them to get off the elevator. I took a deep breath, and then I opened the door.

"Hey Guys," I said, greeting Darren and J.B. at the door. "Come in."

"We had a few stops to make and Jamal had to get settled into his hotel," Darren said as he sat down on the couch.

"You as well," I said as I looked at Darren and then back at J.B. quickly.

"How was your flight?" I asked as I sat down.

"Great," J.B. replied.

"You guys hungry?" Darren asked abruptly.

"A little," I nervously responded.

"I'll go and get the three of us subs," Darren insisted. "While I'm gone, you two could catch up on college days."

"Sounds fine with me," I said, trying to appear calm.

"Yeah, that's cool. Excellent idea Darren," J.B. replied, with a mischievous grin on his face.

"Okay I'll be back in about twenty minutes," Darren said, as headed towards the door.

For a few moments, there was complete silence in the room. J. B. made the first move and began to open up the lines of communication.

"So, did you get the package I sent you?" He asked.

"Yes I did. That was very thoughtful of you."

"Have you given it any thought? I mean you understand why I couldn't be with you in college right?" J.B. asked as he moved over next to me.

"Well in a way I do," I began. "But, I'm not sure if we could ever make it work."

"I know that this isn't easy for you. It sure hasn't been for me, but I had to let you know that I care about you."

"Yeah I know but you know our families will never accept the both of us."

"I know. It's not that easy... I thought this thing would have turned green by now." J.B. said as he tossed my keys in the air.

I couldn't believe that he remembered my old fraternity key chain that I dropped the day I met him in the dorm. I noticed the shine from J.B.'s ring on his finger next to his left pinkie finger. I wondered if he was married so I began to ask him even though I knew the answer.

"J. B. are you married?"

"Yeah I am married. Jay, I don't know why I decided to wait all these years to tell you how I feel. Like I said in the letter, I always wanted to tell you but at that time I'm not sure I was ready. I love my wife, I really do but.... I can't keep lying to myself."

"What do you mean you can't keep lying to yourself? You've done a great job all these years."

"Well, I have always known that I was bisexual, but I never could admit it. I guess you could say getting married was to cover up my hidden lifestyle. And besides…you know my parents are Pastors man. They would disown me if they ever had an inkling that I swung the other way, man!"

"Yeah you are the son of a preacher man and so am I," I joked. "How long will you be in town?"

"For a while, I hope."

"What does your wife think about you being here for that long?"

"We decided to separate for a while; I had to leave her. I had to get away from the south and come back home to New York to kind of clear my head. Besides I have hurt her enough by not being honest. I just could not allow myself to have her look at me everyday knowing I destroyed her life."

"You really love your wife, don't you?" I said as I bit the hangnail piercing the cuticle on my right index finger.

"Bridget is everything to me, but I can't continue to lie to her. She deserves someone who will truly love her," J.B. said, as he laid his head back on the sofa.

"Give me time to think this through. I'm not sure I can just jump into a relationship right now. This all is still a shock to me J.B.," I said. I hesitated for a moment before continuing. "Plus, I am trying to practice being a better Christian now, and this does not line up with the word of God."

"Just give it some thought. Maybe now is the perfect time for us to be together."

"No. The best time was years ago, but you didn't have time. And now you just want to come up in here and change my entire life."

"I guess I had that coming huh? I know that you feel rejected, but I have not rejected you man. I just needed some more time to get where we are now. I was the star of the basketball team at Terminus for God's sake. I could not just come out and say I was in love with you. As harsh as that sounds it is true and I made a big mistake. While I'm here I can give you all of me. Just give me a chance Jay, please." He pleaded.

The door opened and it was Darren with our food. Like I said before he had a key to my place and since he was already at my house I guess he decided to use the key instead of me buzzing him upstairs.

"We'll talk later, okay?" I said as Darren shut the door.

"Sorry I took so long. That place was just so packed. It's a real popular place," Darren said as he threw me my sub.

"That's okay. Did you get me a meatball sub?" I asked.

"Yeah, and a large Cola." Darren said laughing.

"No idiot. I like apple juice," I said as I looked in the bag.

"I'm just playing. I did get the apple juice. Here you go man."

The three of us sat at the table in my dining room and talked about college and what we have been doing since then. Darren and J.B. discussed a new case and their upcoming audit. The life I had secretly kept locked away was starting to somehow come back to haunt me with J.B. showing up on the scene. There was a certain irony in J.B. being the auditor for Darren's firm. And by Darren and I being best friends and so close yet he never knew about the real deal with J.B. I somehow still think that all of this is linked. I was afraid of facing the truth, and the truth was that I was not who my friends and loved ones thought I was. I have been living behind a mask for so long, that if I did not come clean I'm certain that it would be a matter of time before my true identity is revealed. Time had gone by so quickly until I did not realize the three of us had been talking for over five hours.

"Well it's getting late," Darren said. He must have seen me looking at the clock on the wall.

"Where are you staying?" I asked J.B.

"Oh the Hilton on Forty Second Street in Times Square until next week. I'm looking for a place as soon as possible."

"Well I could introduce you to one of my friends who can show you a few condo's for sale. Maybe she could help you find a place." I offered.

"That would be nice Jay."

"I'll see you tomorrow," Darren said.

"You both have a goodnight," I said, as I walked them to the door.

Trying to live right and do what I thought was best for me was so very hard to do. It seemed as if the harder I prayed, the more vulnerable I became. I needed something stronger to help me ease the pain I was feeling, so I went to the kitchen and poured myself a glass of wine. One glass became five glasses, and again for another night I found a way to escape my reality. Soon I became sedated in the intoxication of the wine as it served as my soulful comforter.

Chapter 5

"Good afternoon, Sheila," I said as I walked into my office.

"Good morning, Dr. Phillips. How are you today?"

"Well, I didn't get much sleep last night and I have a headache. But I'll take a few Aspirin and hopefully the pain will go away. I got a late start this morning and I hope I didn't miss any appointments. What time does the Sanders couple come in today?" I called, as I turned on my computer.

"I believe in a few minutes, Dr. Phillips. Let me double check."

"Thanks Sheila," I said as I checked my e-mail. To my surprise, I had nothing in my mailbox, which is rather unusual for me. I then decided to check my messages on my home phone. I checked the messages on my home phone once a week because my friends and family mostly call my cell phone. There was nothing, except for a salesman asking if I needed a new heating system in my house. "Don't think I will keep this one," I said to myself and deleted the message.

"Dr. Phillips, Mr. and Mrs. Sanders are here now to see you actually," Sheila said as she entered my office. I positioned myself in a chair near the sofa where they would be sitting, and pulled out my yellow tablet to recap their session.

"Hello Mr. and Mrs. Sanders. Please take a seat." I said as I closed my office door. "How was the trip?"

"It was excellent," Mrs. Sanders said with a smile on her face. "George and I really realized how much we mean to each other."

"Good, but this is just the first step. You both really need to see how you get along together at home. I think I have a system that could help your marriage. Every week both of you need to come up with things you can do together. Like going to the movies, painting the house, or even going to a fancy restaurant. This will bring the spark that you had in the beginning of your marriage back.

"Maybe that isn't such a bad idea to try and do new things every week together. You are absolutely right Dr. Phillips," Mr. Sanders said as he squeezed Mrs. Sanders' right hand.

"Good, I'm glad to see that you two are being more compassionate. Compassion plays an important role in a marriage. I also am glad that you are thinking about your children. However, I don't want you both to pretend that you really love each other when you don't. What I mean by that is I have seen a lot of couples stay together for the sake of their children, or because they don't want friends and loved ones to know that they are not happy. Staying in a relationship just to please others is not always the best practice. So I hope that you two are being genuine and also sure that you want to stay together."

"I love my wife so very much. And I let the woman I have been seeing on the side go because I want to make my marriage work. When I look at my daughter and my son everyday I think of what I am doing to them, and also what I am doing to my wife by cheating. I have seen the father absent in so many homes in today's society. I just don't want to have my children not having a father around. I am making my marriage work because my wife is a good mother. She has been loyal and faithful to me, and I knew from the day I saw her that I wanted to spend the rest of my life with her." Mr. Sanders said.

"I feel the same way about him Dr. Phillips," Mrs. Sanders agreed.

"That is an amazing turn around since you first started with me a few months ago. I am proud of your progress and I will see you both next session."

"Again thank you so much Dr. Jackson," Mr. Sanders said.

I walked them to the door and sent them on their way with my blessings. As I was heading back to my desk, J.B. crossed my mind. I pulled out the card he gave me with his number on it. I struggled back and forth as to whether I should call or not. But moments later I found myself dialing his number. After two rings he picked up.

"Good afternoon. Jamal speaking." He answered clearing his throat.

"Hey, I just wanted to call and say hello. This is Jay," I said.

"Oh, I wasn't expecting your call so soon after we talked last night. What's up man?"

"Are you free to meet me today for lunch?" I inquired, trying desperately not to sound too anxious.

"Yeah, I can meet you now if you would like."

"How about Gayle's Soul Food restaurant on Forty-Third Street. Do you know it?" I asked.

"I know exactly where that is because I went there the last time I was in town twice. I'll be there."

"Great! I'll see you in a few."

"Jay you are headed for self destruction. This is a warning," I heard a small still voice say to me. I looked around my office to see where the voice was coming from. But there was no one there. I knew I needed some sleep because now I was hearing things. I became very afraid that if I didn't get some rest then I would be hallucinating next. Shelia left early today to take her son to the eye doctor. Before she left she informed me that I didn't have anymore clients to see today. Lately I have only been seeing one or two clients a day. I would normally see four to five clients a day, but I have reduced the number of cases I would take on. Dealing with my client's problems as much as I used to seem to make me even more depressed. However, if I didn't get my act together soon I am sure I would find myself jobless. Sheila depended on me to employ her and I think that is the only reason I have stayed in practice as long as I have. I put the Sanders file away, grabbed my car keys, and headed off to meet J.B. When I got inside the restaurant I spotted him right away and immediately went over to where he was sitting. My heart started pounding, and I could feel a cold drench of sweat starting to form under both of my arms.

"Hello Jay." J. B. said.

"Hey, what's up?" I nervously replied.

"I am just very, very glad to see you. This is a good place to eat huh?"

"They also have good poetry and jazz concerts here as well. The food here is very good. It's one of my favorite spots to come to when I need to escape it all. "

"Yeah. I heard that this new poet by the name of Ron Deheem was in here a week ago. I saw that brother perform at this club in Atlanta at the Underground. He has skills man."

"I saw him when he was here last month at a poetry event in Brooklyn. He makes me want to dig deep into my journal and do some of my own poetry."

"What would you write about?" J. B. asked.

"Oh, stuff about God, love, and keeping secrets." I said.

"Deep man, I could dig that. You should read me some of your work."

"I might, but right now I am ready to eat. How about you?" I asked trying to change the subject.

"Yeah, me too! I'm starved," J.B. replied.

"The lunch buffet is one of the reasons I come here," I said as I pulled away from the table.

I was getting some mashed potatoes when I heard the voice again say to me, *"Don't fail this test."* I was starting to think I was crazy because the person warning me still did not reveal who they were. I then realized moments later that the voice I was hearing was God. He had been warning me all this time not to indulge in anything personal with J.B. that I would regret later. I needed to gain control of my emotions, because if I didn't I'm certain that I would soon give into him. As I returned back to the table I could feel my heart pounding even harder.

"That looks delicious," J.B. said as I placed my plate on the table.

"I told you that the food here is amazing," I replied as I closed my eyes and said grace.

"You're very spiritual," he observed.

"Yes. I always honor the Lord. Whenever I eat something, I have to give Him thanks."

"That church stuff isn't real for me man. God stopped caring about me a long time ago," he said as he squeezed his napkin tightly.

"Look J.B., God knows what you are going through. It took me a while to realize that, but He understands. I went to church Tuesday night and received a word of encouragement from God through my Pastor. So that should be enough evidence that God actually does hear us when we pray."

"Maybe God does hear you, but I don't know if He hears me. I now understand what those guys in college were going through, the ones dealing with their sexuality that is. They couldn't help it. I just feel bad because I would laugh and make fun of them when I was with my boys. But I was the one living in denial. I was really making fun of myself because when I saw them," he began to confess as a tear rolled down his left cheek. The tears held him back from saying another word as I continued to counsel him on what to do next.

"J.B., dealing with your sexuality and restoring your faith is a process. I'm embarrassed by all of this. I'm scared of rejection too. And to tell you the truth, I want to tell my mother and sister. But I've realized that now isn't a good time."

"Why can't you tell your family? I thought you guys were close?"

"Well, my sister is getting married before Christmas, so I'll have to wait. I don't want them to be upset. They might accept it. But if they don't, I wouldn't be able to live with myself."

"I understand where you're coming from. Maybe telling your family is not a good idea right now."

"My sister will probably understand, but my mother will take it hard. She is a minister, and knowing her she would more than likely prescribe prayer to aide my plight. Now don't get me wrong, I believe in the power of prayer, but I'm still not sure I understand some things. I have tried praying and look where it has gotten me. It got me no where! No where J.B.," I said as I twirled the carrots around on my plate with my fork. My voice began to crack as I tried to fight back the tears. I wanted to cry and just let everything that I had been holding back inside of me explode.

"Maybe I should go. When I agreed to eat lunch with you I did not expect to go the religious route. The last thing I need to hear about is some God I am not even sure exist. All of this is a lot for me to digest. Can I call you later?"

"Yeah I'll be home. I'm not doing anything except for looking through some office work I need to catch up on. What are you doing later?"

"Well I thought maybe I could come by."

"Sure, what time?"

"Well it is four o' clock now, so I'll be by in an hour or so," J.B. said as he pushed his chair under the table. "Be home."

"I'll see you then," I said.

I went to the restroom at Gayle's to wash my face, and then I left as soon as I finished. On the ride home I decided to stop fighting between what was good and bad for me. I was burning inside with lust and my desires were overwhelming until I no longer had anymore control. I felt I had suffered enough and I did not want to spend my life old and alone. When I got home I went straight to the refrigerator to eat some ice cream, and then I called Denise to see if she was still going to Tonya's wedding with me. I thought that hearing her voice and eating my favorite ice cream would satisfy my urges. Maybe I would call the whole thing off with J.B. and tell him not to come over. Denise and I were first lovers, first everything, and she was my remedy right now before I made a big mistake.

"Hey Denise," I said as I put the top back on the ice cream carton.

"How have you been?" She asked.

"I have been okay, thanks for the concern. I am also just finishing eating some ice cream."

"Um, that sounds tasty. What kind is it?"

"Chocolate," I said licking the ice cream off the spoon.

"Jay, let me call you back. I have a business call on the other line. I really do want to talk to you but I have to take this call."

"Before you go, I just called to see if you were still going to the wedding with me next month."

"Ah...let me get back with you on that. My schedule has been so hectic, but I promise I will let you know tonight Jay."

"Okay, I'll talk to you later Denise."

I wished that Denise and I could have talked longer but she said she had to take the call. I thought about calling Darren, but I realized that he was still in New Jersey at a meeting. I sat at the kitchen table for an hour doing my budget, office work, and making arrangements to attend my sisters wedding. I tried to keep myself occupied as the food I was heating up was ready for serving. As I was turning the oven off, I heard the buzzer downstairs. It was J.B. I hadn't realized that time had gone by so quickly. It seemed as though I just left him a minute ago. I pressed the button to allow him to enter the building as I raced around my condo making sure everything was in place for his arrival. I went to the CD player and turned on a jazz album. I then grabbed two glasses from the wet bar in my entertainment room, and I checked myself out in the mirror to make sure I looked my best. The doorbell rang and there he stood with a wide grin on his face, and I could see that he was very thoughtful because in his left hand he had a bottle of wine. He came inside and placed the bottle of wine in the ice bucket on top of my wet bar.

"Um something smells good in here," he uttered while he casually draped his coat across the bar stool. He continued to sniff the air as he found his way to the sofa.

"Oh yeah!" I called out trying to be casual and unsuspecting. "I was just re-heating this Cajun casserole I made the other night."

When I reached the bar I tried to let my banter cover up the fact that his coat had its proper place in the coat closet in the foyer. I mean, after all that's what it was for. I continued trying my best not to sound like I was some nervous teen on a first date.

"I found this recipe in Ebony a while ago and decided to give it a try. I don't get to cook as often as I would like to." I made it to the sofa with all of my dignity in tack as I sat next to him.

"Oh, so you can cook, huh?" He asked with a renewed interest. I could all but see the light bulb turn on above his head giving way to a bright idea.

"Now I could get used to that." His voice swelled a little and the idea turned into presumption.

"Yeah, I bet you could!" I retorted defensively.

"My bad! I was just making a joke. You know to lighten up the mood. So you expecting some visitor's tonight?" He tried to sound apologetic yet I could still pick up a vibe of preconceived notions set in motion by him. Perhaps he thought of a devilish plan before he arrived to see me tonight.

"No, Denise is working late, and Darren is still out of town. Why do you ask?"

"Perfect," J.B. said licking his lips.

"Perfect huh?" I echoed as my face began to form pockets of sweat. I felt trapped. His presumptions were no longer cute little hints. His actions were perceived yet still unexpected.

"Let me show you," he said, pulling me towards him.

As he gripped my waist with both of his hands I could feel the heat coming from J.B.'s body. He then kissed my lips and then my neck, and I felt some tension release as my mind, body, and soul became lost in complete ecstasy. Before I knew it we both had stripped, and I was no longer in control anymore. After three hours together, we finally finished. I suddenly became convicted of sin and regretful for what I had just done. I felt a knot in my throat begin to form, and I wanted to cry but I couldn't. I was too embarrassed to let anything out, and my emotions turned into an emotional paralysis as I tried to release the pain. I began to think I had failed God and myself. I needed to be alone so I could try and collect my thoughts. And the only way to do that was to ask J.B. to leave.

I eventually found the strength to ask J.B. to leave. He seemed confused as to why I would ask him to leave, but I did not give him a clear explanation. I felt he had done enough damage and I was not prepared for him to do anymore.

"Is everything okay?" J.B. asked.

"I didn't want things to go this far." I replied.

"What do you mean Jay?"

"God does not like any of this. All of this is not His will. I want to be with you but then I want to please God first. My mother used to say you can't serve two God's, and I think she is absolutely right. I drink night after night so I can escape my pain. I even try to block out the fact that I am attracted to men, that I am attracted to you. So I need you to leave now because I can't do this anymore."

"Look, I love you, and I don't care about what anyone says. Why is it that we have to keep trying to please everyone else? Haven't we both suffered enough?"

"No, J.B. I can't do this."

"When I'm with you I find hope and peace, something my wife... something my wife could never give me."

I walked J.B. to the door and then told him to give me some space. As I watched him walk down the hallway and then vanish in a matter of seconds, I became torn inside. I also felt like a hypocrite. I went to the bar in my entertainment room and drank two rounds of Scotch. I have been married to alcohol for almost ten years now, and the difference between it and people is it never has let me down.

Chapter 6

"WELCOME TO INTERNATIONAL AIRLINES. How may I serve you today?"The representative asked.

"I purchased one round trip first class ticket under the name of Dr. Jackson Phillips on my American Express card," I said as I pulled out my identification card.

"Okay Dr. Phillips, I see on the screen that you are on Flight 489 leaving out of LaGuardia airport New York, New York at 10:00 a.m., arriving at Hartsfield-Jackson Atlanta International airport in Atlanta, Georgia at 12:20 p.m. And that is a first class seat, correct?"

"Yes, that's correct." I said as I placed one more bag on the belt.

"Okay Dr. Phillips, you are all set."

"Thank you! Have a great day," I said, taking the boarding pass from the representative.

I finally made it to the gate and found a seat in the waiting area. I was exhausted from the night before and still had not had a chance to catch up to all that had happened. After J.B. left I resorted to my old habit of trying to drink my way out of a bad situation. When I woke up this morning I found myself on the kitchen floor. I couldn't even make it to the bedroom. I guess subconsciously I didn't want to get in my bed. While sitting in the waiting area, I reclined in one of the seats and pulled out a bagel I bought on the way. As I sat there so many thoughts went through my mind, particularly last night's events. As soon as I was about to open my bottle of apple juice to wash down my bagel, the representative announced that all first class guests could start to board now. I was very exhausted and wanted to get settled in my seat right away. I thought I would have been able to take a nap in the waiting area, but I was sure to get some rest on the plane ride to Georgia.

I got situated and immediately closed my eyes. I hardly had any sleep last night. I began drinking a lot last night and was mad at myself for letting J.B. and I go as far as we did. But I do remember thinking about how Denise would not accompany me to my sister's wedding. I think that she still resents the fact that she and I never wed. In a matter of minutes my body shut down to rest. Just when the sleep was getting good, the pilot awakened me with an announcement.

"Ladies and gentlemen, we have now landed at Hartsfield-Jackson Atlanta International airport. The weather in Atlanta, Georgia is forty-five degrees. There is about a thirty-percent chance of rain, so make sure you have an umbrella. Have a great day, and remember to fly International every time you fly."

It was a short flight so I had a short nap but still woke up with a major headache. Last night loomed over me like a bad dream. Its like someone was pressing the fast forward button because I was just at the ticket counter, then I was eating a bagel, then boarding the plane, and now getting off the plane. It all felt so mechanical almost like an out of body experience. I finally made my way to the baggage claim area to retrieve my luggage.

I was anxious to see my mother and Tonya. I also was very excited to finally be home back in Atlanta as well. Before I could get off the escalator, my mother screamed my name and ran towards me like a cheerleader. My sister was close in tow as she had the look of embarrassment on her face from my mother's cheer. I had to regroup and show no signs of being a little intoxicated still. So I placed two mints in my mouth and put on my reading glasses so they would not see my eyes. If I had on sun shades I'm sure my mother, the private investigator, would ask me to remove them. Once the shades came off she would know what was up with me. I did not feel like having a come to Jesus, confess thy sins, speech from her right now.

"Oh baby, you made it!" My mother said with tears in her eyes.

"One more day to go," I said as I hugged my sister. She had lost a lot of weight since I last saw her.

"Yep' I can hardly wait. I'm so excited, Jay!"

"Where is the groom?" I asked as I looked around.

"Oh Brian is picking up some things, but he'll be at the church tonight for the rehearsal.

"Don't worry. I know you'll like him. He's really a sweet guy." Tonya assured me as we exited the baggage claim area.

On the drive home, I tried to pretend as if I wasn't depressed. I had not heard my mother sing in a while, so I asked her to sing one of the songs she would sing at Tonya's wedding for me. I needed the comfort of her voice to hold me together. As she belted out chord after chord, her voice ministered to me and sent chills all over my body. When we reached home I could see that the house still looked the same. But there were a few changes. For one, the windows were new and the shutters were painted a different color. But no matter what new touches she put to the house the fact of the matter was I was home again.

"Now Jay baby we are going to be in and out, so settle your bags, and be ready in a few minutes to leave for the bridal rehearsal. There's plenty of food in the kitchen, so help yourself," she said as she kissed me on the forehead. "Tonya and I are so happy that you're here."

"It's good to be home. You know I have to be here for my baby sister," I said as I gave Tonya a hug.

As my mother and Tonya went upstairs to get ready for the wedding rehearsal, I decided to call J.B. and see how he was doing. He told me he felt bad after leaving my house last night. He also insisted that we talk face to face when I returned home. I agreed, and told him we would meet maybe for lunch or coffee. I couldn't make the same mistake again. While in the kitchen searching for something to eat, I came across my old yearbook from high school placed on the counter. I had reason to believe my mother had been going down memory lane and forgot to place my yearbook back on my desk upstairs. As I placed the yearbook back on the counter, I smiled, and then exhaled. Being home was a very good thing for me. There was so much love and joy being here in Georgia. The food was superb, and from the many helpings of food I consumed I knew I had missed my mothers cooking. My aunts, cousins, and a few other family members showed up minutes later to help Tonya.

I sat at the kitchen table and watched Tonya run back and forth upstairs and then downstairs. She was nervous and excited, but more-so nervous as she made sure she was ready for the rehearsal. She eventually came downstairs for a while and showed me her dress, which was breathtaking. My aunt Jewel and cousin Barbara helped Tonya with getting all her props for the wedding rehearsal into the car. Tonya had an early bridal rehearsal this afternoon, and later this evening we all would come back to my mother's house and have a family party. When we finally reached the church, I could see a wealth of cars parked in the parking lot. Tonya had a wedding party of about fifty people. Brian and Tonya are very popular here in Atlanta and at the church. Brain also has a very large family, with a total of six brothers and seven sisters.

My sister loved the fact that she had so many new extended family members being that our family was much smaller. I just hope she does not produce more than two or three nieces and nephews for me. I could not keep up with all of their names if she had more than that. I could tell who Brian was before Tonya introduced me to him because he was waiting at the side door of the church with a smile on his face. I had always talked to him on the phone but we had never met in person, nor had I seen any pictures of him. He was very tall, with caramel colored skin, long well manicured dreadlocks, and a regal smile, which accented his snow white colored perfectly, aligned teeth. He also appeared very toned. In other words, the two of them were going to produce me some cute nieces and nephews.

"Hi. You must be Jay," Brian said as he helped me with one of the bags I was holding.

"Yes I am. Nice to finally meet you, Brian."

"You as well man. Your sister has talked about you so much, and since I travel so much it has been hard to lock in a date to fly out and meet you. But thank you for your blessings to marry your sister."

"I feel honored to give her away to you, but treat her right. You have a good woman on your hands man."

"Jay I know that. Everyday I thank God for sending me this beautiful treasure bro."

"Good to hear you say that."

"Places everyone," my mother announced.

Brian and I agreed to continue our conversation later. I meant what I said to him about treating Tonya right. I know that Tonya and Brian have not been together that long so I was a little apprehensive about his sudden gesture to marry her. But if she is happy and she feels she wants to marry Brian then I support her.

Everybody was in his or her positions and the minister asked for me to take Tonya's hand. I was the one that would walk my baby sister down the aisle and then give her away to Brian. We grew up without our father being in our life, and I know that her wedding day is special for her. I just wished that my father could be here for her instead of me. But we have done fine without him in our lives. I call him from time to time, but he is always on the move. Tonya and I have learned to cope with him not being around, but I think it has been harder on my mother than for Tonya.

After the wedding rehearsal everyone headed back to my mother's house for the family party. My mother and Brian's mother and father thought that it would be a good idea for both families to have a gathering before the wedding. Brian's mother and father are Pastors, and raised Brian under the Christian faith, which was very good for my mother to know. How Brian got past her security questions and constant investigations ceases to amaze me. But I think my mother just didn't want her only daughter's heart to be broken like her heart had been broken by our father. The reality is we have to pray that Tonya and Brian never divorce, but we can't control any of that. But from the looks of things it seems as though they both will have a robust future together.

Brian and I talked for a while about what colleges we went to and our careers. I didn't know that Brian owned his own company. He had started an international pre-paid wireless business called *O-Tron*. His company was now serving all fifty states, and ten international countries. That was very impressive and also reassuring to me that Tonya and my future nieces and nephews were going to be secure financially. Brian reached behind the sofa and pulled out a maroon and gold paisley covered gift box with a peach ribbon on top of it, and then handed it to Tonya.

"Oh, what is this?" Tonya asked with a suspicion of surprise on her face.

"Open it baby," Brian requested.

And just as a good wife to-be does Tonya obeyed his command and opened the box. Inside was a small heart-shaped necklace with several diamonds, and in the middle, a sparkling ruby.

"Baby," Tonya said with tears in her eyes.

"Tonya, you are the reason that I live. You are my morning and my night. Tomorrow is going to be more than a ceremony. It's going to be a celebration of the both of us spending the rest of our lives together, forever. I never thought I could find my soul mate, and then there came you. You were sent out of heaven and through time to be here with me here on Earth. There is not a day that goes by that I don't know just how lucky I am to have you in my life. I'm not perfect, but what I can reassure you is that I can give you honesty, protection, and the assurance of knowing that I will always take care of you."

"Come here Mr. Daniels." Tonya said as she grabbed Brian's tie and pulled him closer to her lips.

"Let's make a toast everyone," I said as I raised my champagne flute. "To my baby sister and her fiancé, the future Mr. & Mrs. Brian Daniels."

Brain and Tonya danced to Mary J. Blige's version of *"You Are Everything."* As I watched them dance tears began to fall down my face, and then I felt someone tap me on my back as I wiped my face.

"Come here boy, Mama is in the mood to dance with her handsome son," my mother said as she guided me onto the dance floor.

The festivities finally gave way to the passing of the evening's hours, and the guests began to dissipate until they were all gone. My mother and I set the task of cleaning up and finally waved the white flag of surrender. She retired for the night, and I joined my cousins in the family room. My youngest cousin Ryan was majoring in psychology at *Bayard University,* and it was my hope that he would follow in my footsteps. It would be something to have two doctors in the family. He always called me "Uncle Jackson" since I was older than the other cousins, and because his mother and I were so close. My days as an undergrad at *T.U.* were dancing in the forefront of my thoughts as he spoke of his life at *Bayard.* There was a warm glow in my spirit as

I reflected on those times. Two movies had played and ended leaving tired bodies scattered amongst the sofas, chairs, and even the floor. I surrendered to the softness of the pillow underneath my head, as I drifted away from the scene of my family gathered once again in this house. I was home.

Chapter 7

I opened the closet in my old bedroom and retrieved my wing-collared poly-cotton white shirt, with accented black buttonhole cuffs. I stared at myself in the mirror and saw the image of a man who had fear and sadness in his eyes. Denise and J.B. were on my mind as my emotions ran its own roller coaster course. My mind took me back to when Denise and I were together back at **T.U.** and when I would see her each morning before class.

Before our broken engagement, we would sit in each other's arm on the steps of the library after class and talk about our future. We were so close that we could talk about almost anything. But I never could bring myself to tell her of the inner conflict I faced especially when J.B. came around. Even though we remained friends, Denise has struggled with our break up. I'm sure that's why she didn't want to come to Tonya's wedding with me this weekend. I snapped back to the matters at hand and headed to what used to be Tonya's room where Brian and the other men in the wedding party were getting ready. Tonya and all the female participants were at the church.

"Are you nervous man?" I asked Brian as I entered Tonya's bedroom.

"Yes a little," Brian said fumbling with his tuxedo. "I just hope everything goes smoothly."

"Everything will be great. Hey, you treat my baby sister right or you will hear from me." I demanded.

"Tonya is everything to me man. I have never been in love like this before."

"She is a special jewel Brian. I'm glad she found you man. Welcome to the family!" I said as I gave him a brotherly hug.

"I promise I'll take care of her," Brian reassured me. "Oh God, the limousine is here," he yelled nervously.

"Everybody, downstairs," I called to the other ushers. "Let's go."

We arrived at the church and the number of cars in the parking lot had doubled since last night's rehearsal. The doors at the main sanctuary opened up to the magnificence of the occasion. The glow of candelabras did a soft dance around the room, and the aroma of garden roses in shades of lemon yellow and crimson mingled gently with the creamy hydrangeas. It looked so beautiful filling out the centerpieces, sitting majestically on the stoned columns placed at the head of the pulpit. Tonya's impeccable taste had been carefully honed by my Mother's genteel southern upbringing, decor reflecting the simplistic beauty found in a "less-is-more" ambiance. I quickly made my way to Tonya's dressing room in that the ceremony was about to begin.

"Tonya, are you ready?" I asked as I entered her dressing room.

"Yes. I'm so nervous," Tonya said frantically, and then she took a deep breath. "Okay, I can do this."

"Baby this is the best day of your life. Brian loves you," I said offering my arm. "Now you get it together and show all those want-to-be Divas out there how it's done."

"Jay, I love you," Tonya said as she squeezed my left hand.

"I love you too. This is your day."

"Just wish Daddy was here."

"I'm here for you," I said as I kissed her on the forehead. And off we went as I held her right arm to the church foyer.

Everyone stood in awe when they saw Tonya. She was indeed very beautiful on her big day. Her dress had the longest train I had ever seen, and embedded in the crown of the veil were sparkling diamonds. As we were approaching the altar, Brian looked very nervous. When we reached the altar, I let Tonya's hand go and I joined my mother in the first pew. My mother was crying nonstop beside me as I placed my left arm around her. There was the passing of the rings, the wedding vows, and then the finale of them joining as one union. Before the preacher started to pronounce them husband and wife, they had already kissed. Everyone laughed because you could see that they really were in love, and full of anticipation to be alone.

The ceremony ended in the typical fashion with one hundred guests filing in at my mother's house once again for the reception. My mother had a large back yard and patio area to accompany the large amount of invited guests. Of course there were the photo sessions with the bride and groom, then the parents, then the grandparents, then the bridal party, which seemed to last forever. Dinner gave way to the traditional toasting of the bride and groom to which I had the honor of performing. The champagne flowed and the dancing was inevitable. Wedding celebrations were always a blast. After taking a brief turn with Tonya on the dance floor, I decided to give my mother a twirl or two. We really hadn't had much time alone all weekend. And I hoped I could find a moment to talk to her before I left. I felt so burdened with my secret, that I knew I had to talk with her about it, but not now not tonight. As we danced suddenly, my mother gently pulled away from me and then looked me right in my eyes.

"Okay, what's up Jay?" She asked in that "You better tell me the truth boy," tone all mother's seem to have. Her sudden inquiry startled me and I stammered.

"What? Nothings up Ma! This day has been incredible. Tonya looked fantastic, and I'm having a ..."

"Cut the crap son!" She interrupted. "I know how Tonya looked, and everybody is having a good time and all that. But boy, you can fool them, but you sure can't fool me." Her voice commanded my immediate attention. "I'm your mother and I know when something's not right with you. So out with it now! What is it? Is it that high and mighty job of yours? I know helping those crazy folk is likely to make you feel a little cuckoo yourself."

"No Ma!" I laughed nervously. "The job is fine, and we don't call anyone crazy or cuckoo. This isn't the time or the place we can talk later, maybe tomorrow."

"No, we are going to talk right now and get to the bottom of this boy. Something's on your mind and it needs to be said. You meet me on the back porch now. Just you and I, and we'll get to the bottom of this." I didn't attempt to struggle or fight her because I knew I couldn't win.

"Alright," I surrendered as I found myself walking behind her pressing though the crowd. I took a deep breath and then sighed at the release of stress I had inside of me for such a long time. As my approach grew nearer to tell her I started to panic, so I sat down on the swing set as I rocked myself and looked away. My mother stood in front of me with both of her hands on her hips as her posture demanded a confession out of me. I slowly started talking to her but I never made eye contact.

"Ma I love you so much," I slowly began as tears streamed down my face.

"What is it, Jay? Why are you so upset?" She quizzed.

"I can't do this anymore. I don't know what I want anymore," I continued. I could not believe that what I had been waiting my whole teenage life to do was finally about to happen. But this was not the place or the time. However, I had to tell her but I did not want to do this on Tonya's wedding day.

"What are you trying to say to me boy?"

"When I was eleven years old you started letting me go to Virginia during the summer time to stay with Cousin Harold, and Cousin Pearl. Cousin Pearl would normally work the night shift, and Cousin Harold and I would be the only two at home." I stopped.

"What are you trying to tell me son? Just tell me what happened!" My mother demanded.

"Ma, Cousin Harold hurt me. He hurt me mentally, physically, and sexually. He said if I ever told you he would kill me. I never told anyone until now. I have been battling with this for so long now. I just did not want you to think I was crying out for attention because daddy was never around. This is why I could not marry Denise and this is why I moved to New York to escape it all. But the more I tried to forget what he did to me, the more I would drink. And Denise and Darren moved to New York to be with me. Darren is my best friend and Denise was almost my wife. But I have never told either one of them any of this because I couldn't, especially not Denise. Cousin Harold ruined my life! He destroyed me!" I screamed.

"Not my baby! No! No!" My mother screamed.

"Ma, I have been secretly dealing with this and I have even tried to commit suicide twice. But Ma I couldn't."

"No Jesus! Why? Why my baby? No!" She yelled as she continued to question God.

My world became still as my mother and I stared at each other. She stared at me in a state of shock, and I stared at her in shame. After so many years the burden I have carried for so long was now released. I could not stand to see her cry. She cried so much until her makeup started to drip down her face. The God she had known all her life and the older cousin who raised her seemed to have forsaken and betrayed her. Her endless pleas with God became overwhelming to my ears, as I tried to shake the fact that she now knew my secret. The pain and agony flooded me simultaneously like a tsunami as I tried to deal with my plight head on. My mother raced inside the house as I quickly trailed behind her tracks of disbelief. She went upstairs to her bedroom, and when I reached the last step leading to her bedroom door, I was going to go into her room, but I stopped. However, I found the strength to knock on her door even though my mind played a constant tug of war of if I should or not. After a few knocks, and my tireless requests for her to open the door, she finally acquiesced.

"In the back of my mind I always knew son something must have happened to you, I just was unsure as to what I knew for sure." She began as I sat next to her on the bed. "I raised you and your sister to trust in God no matter what. I raised you the best I could. I was a single mother and twenty three when I had you. It was hard because I would try to be a good wife and mother. Your father would hit me and come in drunk all the time. Then he would always blame me for messing up his life. He would tell me that having two children was a mistake. But I decided to raise my babies. I made it through college, and with the help of Darren's mother and father I was able to send you to school. I tried to do the best job I could. I just should have been more protective. I should have saved you. Why could I have not saved you? Why? Maybe if I listened to your father you would still have him in your life right now. It's my fault! Dear God I did this, I should have been a better mother."

"It's not your fault. Ma, please don't cry." I begged.

"I should have protected you. I am so sorry that you had to deal with that all by yourself. I should have been there. But don't you worry I am here now, I am here now." She reassured me.

The fact of the matter was she was already twenty years late. The damage had already manifested itself using my mind as its host for complete destruction. As my mother rocked me in her arms, I felt safe again. I felt that what she vowed to do, which was to protect me now, was very much sincere. She stopped crying and then whispered in my ear, "Everything is going to be okay, baby." She then began to sing to me *"His Eye's on the Sparrow."* As she belted out chord after chord, bringing me to full deliverance, suddenly it seemed as though the world had stopped. My mother and I were the only ones in unison playing to the beat of redemption.

"Ma, I love you," I said as I wiped her tears with my hands.

"I love you too," she whispered, as she wiped the tears from my face.

"Do you want me to tell Tonya?" I asked.

"We need to all sit down and have a family talk, just the three of us. There are some things I want to tell you and your sister that I should have told you a long time ago."

"Don't worry, Ma. I guess you could say it's natural for a mother to react the way you did."

"This is not easy for a mother to hear coming from her only son. It was hard raising a young man all by myself, and I regret that you did not have your father in your life."

"I have forgiven him and you should too Ma."

"All I can do is pray that God gives you full deliverance. You won't overcome this overnight."

"I am going to talk to my pastor when I get back to New York." I said.

"That sounds like it would do you some good. I am glad to know that in the midst of it all God is somewhere in your life."

"You are such an incredible and strong woman. I love you and I am also glad to know that you will never turn your back on me."

"You listen to me...I am your mother and I am always here for you. You are my first child and my only son, and you never have to question my love for you."

"I needed to hear that. I love you." I said.

My mother and I remembered that there was still a celebration going on in her house, and it also was Tonya's wedding reception. So we both got our acts together and walked back downstairs to the party. Neither one of us wanted Tonya to notice that we were gone, and I did not want her to see our mother crying. When I got back downstairs I assured Tonya I would dance with her before she and Brian left for their honeymoon tonight. But before I did I had to make a call to J.B. because he would be picking me up from the airport tomorrow. I had to see him one more time because I made up in my mind that this would be the last time we would ever see each other. I called him and he agreed to pick me up from the airport in the morning. I then went back to where Tonya was and asked Brian if he would let her go so we could dance. As I danced with Tonya, I held back the tears and the resentment I was feeling inside. I often times wished I could turn back the hands of time because if I could, then this moment would be preserved for Denise and I.

Chapter 8

"Jay, are you still planning on leaving today?" My mother asked, as she tapped me on my right shoulder.

"Yeah Ma, what time is it?" I asked yawning as my body begged me to go back to sleep.

"Seven-thirty. You'd better get up. You said you wanted to leave at eight o' clock right?"

"Thanks. I will be ready in a few minutes."

"I cooked some eggs, toast, grits, and sausage. Get up now, so you can eat." She pleaded.

I wished I could have stayed in Georgia a little longer but I had to get back to New York. I have not felt so much peace like this in a while and my trip turned out to be a counseling session, and a much needed vacation. When my mother came upstairs to wake me up, my mind veered back to when she would come upstairs to wake me up for school. Every morning she would call that same line from the kitchen, "Are you planning on getting up anytime soon?" I missed her so much, and I also anticipated her trip to New York for Christmas. Our bond became even stronger on this trip due to my confession, and I promised her that I would never keep anything else away from her again. I packed my clothes, got dressed, and then I headed downstairs to eat a quick breakfast before heading to the airport. I ate a few bites of the breakfast my mother prepared for me, and then I began loading the car with my bags. I had more bags to take back with me then I brought on this trip. More than likely, I would have to pay extra when I got to the check-in counter. I finally got all of my things in the trunk, and I was now ready to head off to the airport.

"Turn the radio on," I said. "I want to hear that jazz station Tonya has been talking about."

"I believe it's that **Cool 103** something F.M., so baby, you're just going to have to find it. All I listen to is my gospel tapes."

"You still listen to tapes? Ma, you have to get up to date with the CD era. 103.5, I found it," I said as I turned the radio up. "I really like this. My sister knows good music."

"You and Tonya are so much alike. Speaking of Tonya, she and Brian are going to try to come up with me to New York for Christmas."

"You didn't tell her yet, did you?" I asked frantically.

"No. She doesn't know. I will let you tell her."

"Maybe I will wait until she comes to New York." I said.

"That would be good because then you can talk to her face to face."

After forty five minutes of driving we finally reached the airport. My mother walked me to the gate and then she hugged me and told me how proud of me she was. I assured her that I would call her when I got home. I reached the ticket counter to get my boarding pass, and to load my luggage. The ticket agent gave me a break by not charging me for the fourth bag. What she did is not likely to happen at an airport, but I thanked God for the small blessing. It's not that I could not afford to pay for the extra luggage. The fact of the matter was that God was attempting to get me to appreciate the small things. We sometimes can get so consumed in the affairs of this world until we often forget to count our many blessings. So, remember to give thanks because somebody else would rather be in your shoes.

While on the plane, I rehearsed internally what I would say to J.B., Darren, and even Denise. I had a check list of the five people who must know first what I was dealing with. I mentally checked off my list who would be the next in line. Each person had a different relationship with me, so each person would react differently. But as bazaar as it may sound, my greatest fear was to tell Denise. I feared telling her because I feel in many ways I had already hurt her enough after leaving her at the altar on our wedding day. That dark, but vivid image still to this day taunts me. My head began to ache, and my body started to shake because I was now landing in New York. As I looked out of the window I could see that the sky was overcast with charcoal colored clouds. And the rain began to fall endlessly leaving no promise to cease anytime soon. I correlated the weather and my life to the same constant parallel of darkness.

My lighthouse had no more power to send out an S.O.S. so that someone could rescue me. I had run out of prayers, and I had cried all I could cry. I was a complete mess, and until I addressed each person that was the cause of my pain, I would never be set free. I retrieved my carry on bag in the luggage bin above my seat, and I immediately dashed to the baggage claim area. I had taken car service to the airport but now I wish I would have driven. This way J.B. would not have to pick me up, but it was too late now to tell him not to pick me up. My eyes searched endlessly for J.B. but he was nowhere in sight. As I was reaching in my pocket for my cell phone, to call him, I felt someone tap me on my left shoulder. When I turned around to see who the person was I discovered it was J.B. standing behind me. I recognized a familiar glow in his eyes like the one I saw when we first met, but my mind was already made up. I had already laid my burdens down, and I no longer had any place for him in my mind and my heart.

"How was the flight?" He asked.

"The flight was fine. Where is the car?" I asked.

"I parked it over this way. Are you hungry?"

"No, I ate on the plane. Are you?"

"Yeah a little. But I'll just pull into a fast food place somewhere."

"You know J.B., I am so sick of hiding who I am," I began. "Isn't it my life? Why can't I live my life the way I want to?"

"Calm down, man. Are you okay?"

"No. How can I be okay? Look at us," I shouted, but I suddenly stopped myself. "I'm sorry this is my second time blowing up at you. Take me home; I need some rest."

"I talked to my wife last week," J.B. said after a long silence. "I told her about us, and she said that she wants a divorce. I don't blame her. Bridgett and I shared so much together. We've been married for seven years now. She doesn't deserve this. Bridgett felt it was best that I come back to Atlanta, so we could talk things over. You understand don't you?"

"I understand J.B. that God wants you to go back to your wife and make it right with her. I have to get myself right with the Lord as well. Let's not discuss this any further, just, just take me home man."

On the route to my house we did not talk any further as I requested. The only thing that could be heard was the car engine and the radio. When he dropped me off at home I gave him a hug and told him that I would have someone help me get my bags upstairs. Carrington was working today and so I asked him to get my bags. When I said goodbye to J.B., I knew deep down inside that we would never see each other again. It hurt me so much to let him go, but I had to so that I could be at peace with my soul. Carrington delivered my bags inside my condo, and I gave him a tip and told him that I would be downstairs later to help him with his research paper. He was working on early childhood development, and I had some books upstairs which I thought would be a great help to him. I reclined on the sofa, and then I called Denise. After two rings she picked up, but I had hoped it would have gone to voice mail. If that would have happened then I would not have to talk to her.

"Hey Denise, how have you been?" I inquired.

"I got a lot accomplished these past few days. When did you get back? And how was the wedding?" She asked.

"It was beautiful."

"Well that's good. Tonya finally jumped the broom. I know my girl was smiling from here to Jamaica."

"Denise, I really need to talk with you," I said, changing tones. "What are you doing tomorrow around lunch time?"

"Nothing. I'm actually free. What time?'

"One o' clock. Meet me at Gayle's."

"No problem. Jay, are you still having that Christmas party at your house this year?"

"Yeah. We can talk about that too. See you tomorrow."

"Okay, we'll talk then. You seemed a little rushed but I will blame it on not getting enough rest. We will catch up tomorrow."

Denise knew that something was up with me, but I would wait and talk to her in person. Confessing to her over the phone was not the best way to tell her. I poured myself a glass of wine while I sang in chorus with the jazzy vocals of Anita Baker's voice. "I apologize, oh baby I do, I apologize, I know I was wrong," I sang to an audience of one wishing deep down inside that these words would make Denise understand.

Chapter 9

"Good afternoon Dr. Phillips. How was the wedding?" Sheila asked as I walked in the building.

"Just great," I said as I looked at the day planner open on my desk. "What time is Jacquelyn coming in today?"

"You rescheduled for her to see you now actually. She should be here in any minute now sir," Sheila answered.

"If you could just hand me her files, I'll review them before she comes in," I said as I walked to the door of my office. Sheila swiveled to the file cabinet, retrieved the file, and swiveled to me. I smiled as she handed me the file containing Jacquelyn's last visit. As I was reviewing my notes, I glanced around the office. I made sure that there were tissues beside her chair, and that the candy jar was well stocked with gummy bears. Those were her favorites.

"Dr. Phillips, Jacquelyn is here to see you. Are you ready to see her?" Sheila asked over the intercom.

"Absolutely. Send her into my office, please." About two minutes later, there was a quiet knock at my door.

"Hello, Jacquelyn," I said as I opened the door for her. "How are you today?"

"I'm fine," Jacquelyn said as she sat down in the chair. I waited a moment to see if she would start. After a few minutes of silence, I opened her folder and flipped to the last page.

"Last time you were here, you said you were having trouble sleeping. Are you still having a lot of nightmares?"

"Sometimes. But mommy says that I shouldn't be afraid." she said as she squeezed her chocolate colored stuffed bear which only had one eye.

"Who is it that scares you in your dreams?"

"Sometimes I see my uncle," Jacquelyn said, beginning to cry.

"What is your uncle doing in your dreams?" I asked gently.

As Jacquelyn told me her story, I tried to gain her trust, without overwhelming her. We spoke about how her uncle's actions made her defenseless and exposed. She also revealed that sometimes she would feel removed from her body, and that discussing it with her mother sometimes embarrassed her. I could see that Jacquelyn could not talk anymore about what had happened to her, so I walked Jacquelyn to the door and I had Sheila watch her in the lobby. I then asked her mother if she would stay so we could talk alone in my office.

"I'm sorry about the confusion last week. We'll try not to double schedule again." She said as she tried to change the subject.

"Oh, that's fine. But let's stay on subject here. As you heard, Jacquelyn said she's still having a lot of nightmares. She's been expressing a lot of fear of her uncle."

"Yes, I've brought the matter to the police now," she said beginning to tear up. "That sick bastard - excuse my language - is finally behind bars."

"I know this is a very difficult time for you, Mrs. Matthews. If you ever feel like you need to talk, I could definitely refer you to a colleague of mine who specializes in these sorts of things."

"Yes, I've thought about what you said last time. I think though I'm going to pursue matters through the church."

"Regardless, it's important for you to provide unconditional support for Jacquelyn. She said a few minutes ago that sometimes she feels embarrassed about talking about it with you."

"Is this normal?" Mrs. Matthews asked, reaching for a tissue.

"Yes, it's often the case that victims feel reluctant to talk with their parents about the details. Just make sure that you remind her that you love her and that when she is ready, she can speak to you about anything."

"This is my baby, my only child. I am torn inside Dr. Phillips," She began to weep uncontrollably as her emotions flooded her. We spoke more about Jacquelyn's progress and Mrs. Matthews appeared to feel responsible for her daughter's molestation. I insisted that she pursue help in some form, whether through her church or through a counseling agency. I also introduced the option of incorporating medication into Jacquelyn's treatment, an idea that Mrs. Matthews vehemently opposed. Though I usually don't advocate its use on children, I found that in Jacquelyn's case, an anti-depressant with a light sleeping aid might have its benefits.

"Thank you so much for everything you are doing for Jacquelyn," Mrs. Matthews said, slinging her purse over her right shoulder.

"No problem," I said. "Just make sure you're taking care of yourself as well."

"Say goodbye to Dr. Phillips," Mrs. Matthews said to Jacquelyn, who was sitting in the corner of the waiting room staring at the ground.

"Bye, Dr. Phillips," she said quickly looking up.

"I'll see you both next week," I said waving from Sheila's desk.

"Isn't she just adorable?" Sheila said, as Jacquelyn and her mother walked down the hall.

"Yes, she is a little angel," I said, tapping the counter with her file as I watched Mrs. Matthews wrap her arm around her daughter's shoulder.

"I'm leaving for lunch," Sheila interrupted my trance. "Do you want me to get you anything Dr. Phillips?"

"No, I'll be eating at Gayle's today with a friend," I said, shaking my head suddenly. "But thanks anyway."

"Okay then," Sheila said, collecting her purse and coat."

As I drove to the restaurant to meet Denise for lunch, I thought about Mrs. Matthew's reaction. I always found it difficult to talk to the parents of my young patients, especially in cases like Jacquelyn's. Their responses reminded me so much of my mother's reaction and pain. After she discovered recently that I was molested when I was younger, she has blamed herself for the act.

Mrs. Matthews told me that she was afraid that Jacquelyn's future relationships would always be marred by this early abuse. As I thought about this fear, I was sure that now, after my revelation about dealing with my childhood pain, my mother felt even guiltier. The things my cousin did to me are hard for me to speak about even now. My mother still refuses to refer to him by name. Instead she uses other profane titles when she speaks of him to me. I left my office and headed straight over to meet Denise at Gayle's. When I arrived I could see that Denise was already inside waiting for me. I suddenly felt a trail of sweat form on my forehead and then on my neck. I was scared and a little uneasy of what Denise's responses might be, but she had to know.

"Hey, Jay. What's up?" Denise said as I walked inside. She was seated on a bench in the lobby.

"Nothing, just a little tired," I said embracing her, and then quickly pushing her back to take a look at her outfit. "Now look at you. Don't you look good today?"

"Thanks. I made this dress myself!" Denise said proudly.

"Well, it's amazing," I said looking around. "Hey let's find a seat. I'm starving."

"Mmm... the smell of soul food," Denise said as we walked to the first available table with the waiter. "So how long was Miss Tonya's dress?" Denise asked as she looked at the menu.

"It was a very long one," I answered trying to make a selection. "A long one that she spent a lot of money on. I really liked the V shaped cut in the front. It was white with pink heart shaped embroideries on the back. And she had green and pink flowers in her hand. She and Brian will be here for Christmas. I'll tell her to bring the pictures along."

"What did you need to talk to me about, Jay?" Denise asked after the waiter took our orders.

"Well Denise what I'm about to tell you will probably be a bit of a shock."

"Okay," she replied crossing her arms. "What is it? I'm listening."

"I'm... I don't know if you're ready for this. Please don't judge me," I said as I took a deep breath. "I'm still the same Jay you have always known."

"Jay, what are you talking about?"

"Denise, I have been living a lie," I said as my heart raced. "Look, if you want to walk away, I understand. I just thought you should know."

"You are scaring me. What are you talking about?"

"I know that you have never forgotten our wedding day. I mean there you were all dressed in white, waiting for your knight and shining armor, and I let you down. Not only did I let you down I let my family down, I let God down, I let your family down, and I even let me down. I love you so much and I am glad that we are still great friends after all that."

"Jay I am over that really. I mean it was very embarrassing to deal with not being your wife, but I still have you. So Jay you don't have to feel bad about that."

"No Denise that is not what I really wanted to talk about. Denise the reason I asked you to lunch today is so that I could tell you what I have been going through all these years. I have had affairs with men every since college, and I can't go on living a lie."

"Oh my God, Jay. This is shocking," she stuttered. "When did this happen, or start, I mean? So this is why you couldn't marry me?"

"Yes and no. I really do love you. But I didn't want to hurt you."

"Does anyone know about this other than me Jay?"

"My mother knows. I told her after Tonya's wedding."

"Did you tell Tonya or Darren yet?"

"Not yet. I don't even know if I should."

"This is so crazy for me to comprehend. I never expected a confession like this."

"Denise," I paused as I saw the hurtful expression on her face. I feared what her next reaction would be to the next part of my confession. "There is one more thing I have to tell you. J.B. and I were involved as well."

"Jamal?" She asked. "The same Jamal that's working with Darren? The guy you both knew in college?" She stammered in disbelief.

I nodded. I knew she was hurt, and I couldn't even bear to look up at her across the table. She knew him as Jamal and J.B.

"What!" She screamed. "This is a nightmare!" She continued in a rage as others stopped and watched us at the table.

"I'm sorry I thought you should know. But I am going to make an appointment with Pastor Clark, so he and I can talk about all of this.

You are such a strong, black woman. I wish I could have been that strong, black man you needed."

"If it is alright with you I must leave now. I need to clear my head and digest everything."

"I understand, and I did not expect for you to be excited in the least bit about any of what I just told you Denise."

I took another gulp of the wine in my glass and tried as hard as I could to fight back the tears that I felt coming down my face. As I watched Denise walk away from the table, I regretted not being able to be her Prince Charming. Though I still loved her, I knew that this alone wasn't enough to build a relationship from. A few minutes after Denise left, I left and headed straight to my office. As soon as I opened my door, Sheila greeted me with a phone call. "Line one," she motioned abruptly.

"Hello, Dr. Phillips speaking," I said as I picked up the phone.

"What's up, bro?" Darren said.

"Nothing," I said, sitting down. "I just stepped back in from lunch."

"How was the wedding?" Darren asked.

"It was good. Tonya finally got her Prince Charming, and I'm happy for her."

"That's great. Listen, have you seen J.B. today?"

"No, I haven't heard from him," I said wondering if he and J.B. had talked about me.

"That's odd." Darren said. "He didn't show up for work today."

"Strange," I said, feigning ignorance. "Look, can you stop by my house tonight on your way home? I have to talk to you about something, man."

"Sure, I'll head over after work," he said. "Are you okay? You sound really anxious."

"I'm fine, but stop by the house, okay?" I said. As soon as I hung up, I was startled again by an incoming call. Sheila peaked in my office and told me that someone was on line two waiting to speak to me.

"Hello, this is Dr. Philips," I answered abruptly.

"Jay this is J.B. Listen before you hang up the phone let me just say that I'm sorry."

"Look," I said. "I'm not mad at you. I'm just hurt right now. I can't talk to you anymore."

"I've been confused myself," he began, but I didn't hear the rest. I hung up and gave a deep sigh.

Talking to J.B. was not going to solve my problems, nor was it going to lead me to full deliverance. If I accepted his calls, I would fall into that pattern of sinful behavior again. All I could do at this point was pray for him. But first, I had to pray for myself. Later that night, when I pulled into the garage, I saw that Darren's car was already in the parking lot downstairs. He must have been around the corner from my house and let himself in to wait for me.

"Hey, Darren," I said, as I opened the door. "You beat me home."

"Hey," he called back from the kitchen. By the sound of things, I could tell he was helping himself to the contents of my refrigerator. I returned my coat and my shoes to their places in the foyer closet. I took a deep breath and felt my heartbeat rising as I walked to the kitchen to join him.

"Where did you get that painting?" Darren asked, as I entered the room. He was seated on a stool at the counter, holding a large sandwich in his hands. He took a big bite and half its contents spilled out the other side onto the plate.

"I got it a year ago when I was in New Orleans at the annual jazz festival," I answered folding up the cuffs of my shirt. "I thought you saw it the last time you were here?"

"I've never noticed it before," he said between bites.

I poured myself a tall glass of water and sat down next to him. I looked at the painting and worried about how I would bring up the topic.

"Didn't you say you wanted to talk?" Darren asked as he wiped his mouth with a napkin. What's up?"

"This isn't easy for me to say," I began, taking a big gulp of water. "Before I tell you, I want you to realize that I'm still the same Jay you have always known."

"Okay bro' I understand," Darren interrupted. "Spit it out already."

"Well, the reason I asked you to come by is," my voice trailed off. "I thought if I told you on the phone, you would just hang up."

"I've known you how long? Just tell me bro."

"I've been secretly dealing with my sexuality. I have prayed and prayed and I did not want to tell you. But I have told my mother and I have told Denise. You were my best man at my wedding, you are my best friend, and I did not want to lose you. I also did not want to make you think for one minute that I was attracted to you in that way. I just felt you would not understand me. That night in church when I was crying as much as I was, that was the reason why. Or the night you kept calling and calling and I would not pick up that is the reason why. I am tired Darren, I can't do this anymore man. I want out of all of this. I want to be free, I want to know that I don't have to go through this by myself," I finally said. I fought to not make any eye contact with Darren. I assumed that his reaction would be one of disgust and shame of me.

Darren stood in front of me and starred at me and never said a word which made me even more frightened. After a few minutes of him looking at me without saying anything, he then took my left hand and squeezed it.

"What's wrong with you?" I asked, stunned at his sudden gesture.

"Don't say another word."

"Say what?"

"I always knew," he said. "I just wondered when you would stop lying to both of us."

"What do you mean you knew?" I asked defensively.

"I saw the chemistry between you and J.B. that night at the table when we were over eating subs," Darren began. He stared into my face and forced me to look at him. "I still remember one night when we were in college, we were having some beers at the frat house and you said that you wished J.B. would notice you. I played it off. I didn't know what was going on. Also too, there are a few things that you have done through the years that I suspected, but I never announced it. I figured you would tell me eventually."

"I don't believe this," I said, shaking my head.

"We're boys," he continued. "We grew up together. That'll never stop. Man, we're family."

"Thanks man," I said getting up to embrace him. "I have nothing but love for you bro'."

Darren and I talked further about my summer in Virginia, how my mother reacted to my confession and more importantly how Denise reacted. He stayed for a while and we both even prayed together. I admired his reverence of God and also for him still wanting to remain loyal to me after all I had told him. After Darren left, I decided to call my mother. I told her about Darren and what a good friend he'd proven to be. She and I talked for an hour and then we prayed together as well. Just as she was telling me to keep my head up, I received an incoming call. It was my sister. I told my mother who said to take the call. I said goodnight and switched lines. I had not talked to Tonya since the wedding and I knew she and Brian were still on their honeymoon.

"Sorry I called so late," Tonya's voice rang clearly through the line. "I just haven't talked to you since the wedding. I miss you. How are you doing?"

"Oh I'm fine, I'm so glad to hear from you. How is married life treating you these days?"

"It's been wonderful. Brian and I could live together forever. And guess what?"

"What?"

"You are going to be an uncle really soon!" Tonya said screaming.

"Get out of here!" I returned. Tears welled up in my eyes. "Congratulations Tonya! How far along are you?"

"It's early, just a few weeks. I know I'm supposed to wait, but I couldn't keep it in any longer!"

"I can't believe this. So wait, that means you were pregnant before the wedding right?

"Yes it does. But that is why Brian and I decided to get married."

"Well I am surprised you have not told our mother."

"She and I will talk when I get back, I told you because I knew you would not chew me out."

"Yeah you know how she is. Are you still coming to my Christmas party?"

"Well, I didn't get a formal invitation yet."

"Are you kidding me? You know you're invited."

"I'm just teasing. We've already booked tickets."

"You'd better be," I said. "But listen, I'm exhausted. Can I call you back in the morning?"

"Definitely. Brian is ready to go to bed," Tonya giggled.

"Um, I'm scared of you lady. Go before you get in trouble."

"You're crazy. We just both have to get up early in the morning silly. We signed up to go on this tour of the island so we have to get up early."

"Bring me something back and have fun. Love you, Tonya. Talk to you later."

Tonya had not told anyone that she was pregnant before the wedding. Knowing my mother, she would have probably given Tonya a speech. But Brian did marry my sister and I guess that is good to know that the baby will have its father around. It made me happy that my sister was doing so well. But on the flip side of things, it made me feel lonelier though. She was no longer dependent on me as she had been for so long. "She has a good man by her side", I thought to myself as I got ready to say my prayers. Finally, the Lord has answered all her prayers. This realization gave me reason to believe my blessing was soon on its way.

Chapter 10

"Good afternoon. I am glad to see the both of you here, today. How are things working out?"

"Just fine," Mr. Sanders replied.

"Yesterday we celebrated twenty years of marriage," Mrs. Sanders said with an assured warm smile.

"I'm glad to see that the two of you are making progress," I said. "It's important to move forward, but not to forget about the troubles of the past. Let's start today with an exercise. Mr. Sanders, would you like to begin?" He nodded."I want you to turn to your wife and express your love for her. I want you do this, however, without using the word love." He hesitated. "Sometimes it's easy to just say 'I love you,' without thinking about what the words mean," I said, trying to help him. "Act as if I'm not even in the room."

"Baby, I'm sorry I've hurt you," he began, turning to face her. "I want to live to see twenty more years with you."

"Let's not dwell on the past, George. Let's look at the now." Mrs. Sanders said.

"I am glad to see that you both finally realize how much you need each other," I said.

We continued our session, with Mr. and Mrs. Sanders taking turns expressing their frustrations and their desires for each other. It was exciting for me to be such a help to others. In a way, it felt like I was a medium through which the Lord could touch His people. I could guide others into His light.

Sending the Sanders on their way, I was in the mood for some good food. I decided to ask Sheila out to lunch with me. We hadn't had lunch together in a few weeks, and the last time we did, we had a great time. We laughed at silly jokes, and talked about issues that most blacks face on a daily basis. I asked her over the intercom, and she agreed to have lunch with me. Two things you will note with me, I am obsessed with time so I am always talking about it, and I love to eat. So I am always one to ask my friends, and business partners to meet me somewhere for brunch, lunch, or dinner. I love to cook but I find it easier to just eat out instead.

We decided to head over to Gayle's of course. I had recommended the place to her a few weeks before and she agreed that it was one of the best soul food restaurants in the city. Since the weather was terrible and I didn't feel like trekking over to the parking garage, we took a taxi to the restaurant. Once inside, I suggested that we sit in my favorite place, over by the window. Sheila and I both decided to try the seafood buffet. The Chef had just put out some fresh catfish nuggets and I was ready to inhale as many as my stomach would allow. The buffet was only open for lunch time, so if you came for dinner you would have to order from the menu.

"When is the Christmas party you are having this year?" Shelia asked, returning to the table with her plate.

"Friday night," I answered between bites. "There will be plenty of food."

"What should I bring? I have to bring something."

"How about one of your delicious apple pies?" I requested.

"I will make sure that I bring my special pies because I know how much you love them. Have you made all the arrangements?" She asked.

"I've ordered red and white flowers, finger foods, and cookies. I think I have it all. I'm looking forward to putting up the Christmas tree with my mother and my sister. My sister is bringing her husband Brian. It's going to be a lot of fun."

"That reminds me of the tradition I used to have with my husband's family." Sheila said as her face painted a sad look.

"Sheila, I really admire you."

"How could a woman on the verge of tears be admirable?"

"You're a caring mother and a wonderful friend. So why are you crying Sheila?"

"I am crying because sometimes it is so hard for me to be a single mother. I also want to start dating again but every since James and I divorced I have not seen any other men. So the holiday times just make me sad and reflect on the way things used to be."

"You should be crying tears of joy not sorrow. When I look at you, I see a woman of great strength and an over comer. You have me and a wonderful son in your life, so that is nothing to be sad about."

"That is so sweet, sir."

Shelia and I sat at the table talking about her son and ex-husband. She spoke about the end of their marriage and what a toll it took on her life. Her husband was going to church for a while, almost every Sunday. Somewhere along the line, however, he started drinking heavily and then started to use drugs. The drugs and the alcohol made him become very violent towards Sheila. I admired her dedication of being a great mother and her professionalism as my assistant. If you met her, you would wonder why someone would treat her that way. Sheila represented the power and strength of a determined strong black woman. After nearly an hour and thirty minutes, I looked at my watch and realized that lunchtime was long over. There were a couple of things I needed to get done, and Sheila had some files she needed to reorganize as well.

"Sorry to cut you off, but I have an appointment today to get to."

"You're right. I believe you have an appointment with your new patient, Jason Avery in a few minutes."

"Yes, my pro bono case. He's at the St. John's Children's Hospital, correct?"

"Let me see," Sheila said, taking out the appointment book she carried with her everywhere. "Yes, he's in room 303."

"Here pay for lunch and here is some money for your taxi." I said as I gave Sheila some money to cover lunch and her taxi.

Since I didn't have enough time to return to the office, Sheila and I parted ways and I caught the first taxi outside the restaurant. I then headed straight for the hospital. I instructed the driver to proceed to East 135th Street.

Before entering the hospital, I prayed to the Lord to give me the strength to help this young boy. Jason Avery had recently lost his mother and had been placed in a large foster home. Some of the other children in the home convinced him that if he died, he would be closer to his mother. After attempting a suicide that drew a lot of media attention, Jason was placed under psychiatric care. I agreed to take on the case after seeing it a few weeks before on the news. Since the state Social Services office worked slowly, it wasn't until now that I could finally meet with him. As I stood in the elevator I wondered what words I could say to Jason that would make a difference in his life. On the third floor I saw a full figured black woman with salt and pepper curly hair, dressed in all white sitting at the front desk. So, I walked over to introduce myself.

"Good afternoon. My name is Dr. Jackson Phillips. I'm here to see a patient by the name of Jason Avery."

"Yes, Dr. Phillips. We've been expecting you. Right this way," She said as she directed me down a long narrow cold hall.

When we reached the front door of Jason's room she slowly handed me a file which contained his medical history. Though I'd already received copies of his file, I accepted it as it might prove to be useful later on during our visit. She told me to let her know if I needed anything. I assured her that I would be fine and entered his room. Jason sat on the floor of the hospital room quietly as if he was expecting my arrival. He was interlocking a set of train tracks in a circular formation as he pushed the black engine around the tracks continuously. He then shifted his weight and turned in my direction to look upward at me as I approached him.

"Hello, Jason," I began as I sat down next to him on the floor. "My name is Dr. Phillips. How are you today?"

"Leave me alone," he answered angrily.

D. J. Coleman

"I know right now things are pretty tough. Though you might not think so, things will get better. You just have to trust me."

"Trusting people is why I'm even in this stupid hospital now. I just wanted to see my mother."

For a moment I was speechless. I hated to see children suffer. I silently prayed that the Lord would walk me through this process. Perhaps I was trying to approach this a bit too aggressively, so I attempted to try a different method. "If you don't want to talk, do you think I could just play with you?" I asked.

He thought about it for a moment, and then he nodded his head in a yes its okay motion. I took some of the tracks from the bin and set them up in a similar circle and then spun the trains around.

"Sometimes our loved ones have to leave this Earth to go to a better place," I began after about five minutes of playing with him. I looked over at him to gauge his reaction. He seemed to hear me but didn't respond.

"Your mother would never leave you on purpose," I continued. "It was just her time to go. You will get a chance to see her again some day. However, trying to hurt yourself is not the way to do that."

"I miss her a lot." He replied.

"What did you do with your mother when you were feeling upset?" Jason stopped pushing the trains around on the tracks. And to my surprise he came over and sat beside me.

"Sometimes we prayed," he replied softly.

"Do you want me to pray with you?"

He answered me and said yes he wanted me to pray with him. I took him over to his bed and we both sat down. I clasped my hands and closed my eyes.

"Father in heaven," I began slowly. "You said that you would not give us more than we can handle. You said you would never leave us nor forsake us. Father, we come now and request that you bring back the peace into Jason's life. We also ask that he understands, as he grows older that you are not hurting him by taking his mother away for she is in a better place. Amen."

"Amen," Jason echoed.

"What are you feeling now?" I said as I pulled out my pen and his file.

"I feel a little better. This place you say Mommy is, where is it?"

"Well, it's way, way, up in the air. God lets us live here on Earth for a while, and then he selects certain people to go ahead of others to heaven at different times."

"So when is my time?" Jason asked, looking at me with sad eyes.

"God is the only one who knows that. God does not want us to harm ourselves, or others."

I began to pack up my things. Our time was already up. Jason took an interest in my cell phone, as I was rearranging my things in my briefcase. I let him play with it while I put my coat back on and pulled my scarf tightly around my neck.

"I will see you next week buddy," I said, giving him a smile of assurance.

"Okay," Jason said, handing me back my cell phone as I replaced it in my upper left pocket on my suit. As I walked to the elevator, I thought about Jason's predicament and how unfortunate it was for such a young boy to be experiencing great pain like that. Although I was not his father, or his older brother, I still felt that I could be that male role model he needed. I made up in my mind after leaving him that I would keep a close watch on him. I did not grow up with too many male figures in my life, so this was my way to make up for what I did not have. After just one hour, I could see a glow in his eyes which meant that I had brought some light to his darkness. So many children across America suffer from abuse or the loss of a parent. I decided that I would make a difference in Jason's life, even if it were the last thing I did. I figured if I could reach just one child then at least one has been saved for today.

I took a taxi and once I got inside I instructed the driver to take me uptown to Jake's a local bar to have a few drinks. As the car maneuvered its way through the evening traffic, I began to see this city in a different respect than I had before. New York is somewhat bitter sweet because many people come here chasing a dream, or killing a dream. My mission for coming here was so that I could run away from religion, my secret life, and my past. But the irony of it all is that I had not run away from anything. God, the mess I had covered up, and my past followed me to New York. Nana Peggy would say, "Jackson baby what is done in the dark will one day come to light. You can't run from

God son, nobody has the ability to do that. When He has His hands on you, there is nothing that you can do except be still and know that He is God. If you ignore His plans for your life, He will allow things to happen so you can better understand Him." I think about her daily and the many things she taught me, and how wise she was. While I was approaching the bar I told the driver to turn the taxi around and take me back to my office. I had left my car there earlier, and I decided that I would not allow liquor to make me its slave tonight. No, you see tonight I wanted to do something different. I wanted to deal with my issues while I was sober. Liquor has always been the easy way out for me, but tonight I wanted my power back. Tonight I wanted to trust in God again. Tonight I could learn to cry, learn to laugh, and learn to face reality without being drugged up.

Chapter 11

WHILE BRUSHING MY TEETH, I turned on the television and watched the Oprah show. Brian McKnight was her special guest and he sang one of my favorite holiday classics, *"Noel."* His music has always been a part of my musical collection, so without hesitation I turned the volume up. My holiday vacation started today, and I was ready to make the most of my time away from the office. Though I still think about my clients during my time off, I realized that I still needed a break for the holidays. However, I always keep my clients in my prayers and I hope that each one of them finds his or her way in life. All I could do was be an ear that listens to them when they needed to vent. And yes, my job is to give them feedback, but it is not so much the feedback that matters, it's how effective my feedback becomes in their lives. It's like if someone gives you pearls of wisdom and you don't utilize those pearls to be a better person, then you have in essence misused those gifts.

I had some rice, potatoes, and ham leftover from last night's takeout that I reheated for brunch. During the week, I barely spent time in the kitchen so this was an intimate moment for me. As my food was warming up in the microwave, I took a look around the kitchen and noticed that I had to put away some dishes and papers. As I cleaned off the counter, J.B. crossed my mind. But then the microwave timer went off, and all I could think about was food. The timer helped me lose focus of him and regain consciousness of repairing my life. With the New Year approaching, I hoped that soon I would be fully delivered from the chains of guilt, depression, and sin finally. My initiative to change my life was my new campaign to win self help and love back into my life. As I inhaled my last potato, I drank some grape juice to wash it all down, and then I left my condo and headed to the dry cleaners. I did not have to go far because the cleaners were right across the street from my condo. I could see that most of the residents in my building were in the holiday mood because most of the doors were covered with trimmings of red and green wall paper. Large wreaths and mistletoe also hung from most of the doors as well. The cold whisk of the winter air made my teeth clutch together as I buttoned up my coat to stay warm. When I got inside the cleaner's the owner greeted me immediately.

"Hi, Dr. Phillips good to see you sir. Are you here to pick up your suit?" The clerk asked.

"Yes. Is it ready yet?" I asked.

"Yes it sure is. I will be back in a minute with it."

"No problem," I said as I looked around the small building. I had been coming to the same dry cleaners ever since I moved to New York. Not only did I like the service, but I also found it important to support family-owned businesses. Whenever I could, I tried to support my brothers and sisters in the black community. Though it was not the most elegant dry cleaning service, I looked past the structure of the building and I saw a black family trying to make a living. I was in the spirit of giving so I thought I would give a nice tip.

"Dr. Phillips, here is your suit. I also was able to get that stain out successfully," the clerk said as she handed me my suit.

"How much do I owe you?"

"Your total is $15.00 sir."

"Here you are," I said, handing her a fifty dollar bill. "Keep the change, and have a happy holiday!"

Back at home, I opened the window halfway in my bedroom to circulate the air. I lit a few candles and watched part of a movie on television. From time to time, I like to smell the freshness of the outside air. After an hour or so, I moved over to my chair by the window after closing it, took out my journal, and began to write. I would not keep the window open for long being that it was cold outside.

I dated the page and titled the entry, *"My Place in this World."* I began:

"God, you have been there for me through the good and the bad. But Lord, when will these feelings of loneliness leave? You have given me material things, a loving family, and a wonderful career. At the same time, I don't have someone to love me. When Denise did not attend Tonya's wedding, I was crushed, and even surprised. After my confession to her I could see how angry she was with me. I messed up, and I think I have lost one of the best things that ever happened to me since you came into my life Lord. What about love? The way she looks at me sometimes makes me feel guilty. Her heart has been broken by the choices I have made in life. When will this all pass away? I am not sure if this letter matters, but I feel better now that I have gotten it out of my system for now.

Sincerely,

Your lost son, Jackson

I was not sure what I was writing in my journal, but it felt comforting being able to release my emotions. Lying alone in bed night after night had become exhausting. When I would roll over, there was no one there. When I would reach out in the middle of the night, still there was no one there. The very thought of it makes me want to just end my life as soon as possible. I am educated, nice looking, and I have a wonderful career but I still can't find anyone that understands me. As I stared out of the window in my room I wished I could one day be content with just learning to love me.

The sound of the phones constant ring snapped me out of my depressive trance. Something within me knew this was an important call. And as I read the caller I.D., that inner feeling was confirmed.

"Can I speak to Dr. Jackson Phillips please?"

"Speaking. Who is this?" I asked.

"Sorry to bother you, Dr. Phillips. I am calling from St. John's Hospital. Jason Avery's grandmother passed away last night. I was calling to see if you could see him today. He will not say a word to any of us."

"Thank you for letting me know. I'll be right over." I said without thinking about if I was going to go or not.

I grabbed my coat and my scarf, and then I raced out the door to go and see Jason. Carrington stopped me to talk but I told him that I had to run. I caught my breath, opened my car, and then I took a deep breath. I started the engine, and off I went to comfort Jason. On my way to the hospital I started to pray for Jason, and then I asked God to use me to minister to him. When I got in the elevator I became very nervous as to what I would say. As soon as the elevator came to a stop, I rushed out and sought out the first nurse I could.

"Good morning, I'm Dr. Jackson Phillips. I received a call this morning stating it was imperative that I see Jason this morning. How is he doing?"

"I tried to give him some breakfast, and he refused to eat. I really feel sorry for him, especially so close to the holidays."

I went into Jason's room and found him sitting in his favorite place on the floor. Slowly, I walked over and sat beside him.

"Good morning Jason. Remember me?" I asked quietly.

"Leave me alone. What do you want from me? There is nothing you can do."

I remained quiet for a while as I gathered my thoughts. I knew that only the Lord could give me the right words to say.

"Are you listening?" I asked.

"I'm listening," Jason said, as he wiped his face.

"I know right now you're upset. This isn't easy, and it's not your fault. God wants you to be strong. It is okay to cry, but it's also okay to smile. You're an intelligent boy, and you have a long life ahead of you."

"Dr. Phillips, am I going to be living with you now?"

"No," I answered honestly. "But very soon, I promise you that you're going to be living with a family that you can trust just as much as you trust me."

"So you're going to leave me too?"

"No, little man. I'll always be here for you, as a friend and a doctor. You're stuck. You can't get rid of me now."

Immediately, I saw a twitch in the corner of Jason's mouth. It quickly disappeared, but I pointed my finger to the spot on his face.

"Was there a smile hiding back there?" I teased.

The nurse brought in a fresh meal tray, and after some coaxing,

Jason nibbled a little on a piece of bread. When he seemed finally settled for a nap, I sought out a nurse in the hallway.

"Excuse me."

"Yes?"

"Could you get me Jason's records? I'd like the number for his case worker."

"Is there something we should be aware of?"

"No, I just need the number," I said in a defensive tone.

"Here's the number," she said, handing me a slip of paper.

I pulled out my cell phone and dialed the number. My intention was to get Jason a family before the holidays.

"This is Paul Brown. How may I help you today?"

"Hello, this is Dr. Jackson Phillips. I've been treating Jason Avery. Are you his case worker?"

"Yes. How can I help you?"

"As you know, Jason has suffered great losses in the last few weeks. It's my professional opinion that the boy should be placed in a foster home as soon as possible. I feel that the hospital environment he finds himself in at the moment is hindering his recovery."

"At this time, we feel that the hospital is the best place for him to be. He has tried to kill himself twice, and he is very aggressive."

"I disagree."

"I understand your concern. But right now, however, we need to keep him where he is at least not a risk to himself and those around him."

"How about trying to release him for the holidays with a relative?"

"That'll be tough. This time of the year, we're really busy."

"I'm just asking you to try."

"I'll try, Dr. Phillips. But please, don't get your hopes up."

"Thank you Mr. Brown." I said as I pressed the end button on my phone.

When I arrived home I put on a jazz album followed by a hot bubble bath. I enjoyed the soothing comfort of soaking in the tub. While I was sitting in my tub, I thought about everything in my life. My party was going to be happening this week, my mother would be coming in the next few days, and of course J.B. was on my mind again. The pain of spending one more night alone began to taunt my relaxed mind once again. I felt myself slowly trying to pick up the phone to call J.B. or Denise, but I did not. It was not fair to face the reality that entertaining anything with J.B. was not of God and that calling Denise would be right.

After about thirty minutes of relaxing in the tub I finally got the strength to get up and dry myself off. I put on my white terry-cloth robe, which hung on the back of the bathroom door. The warmth of the robe made my body feel as soft as silk. I didn't see any need to put on any pajamas until I went to bed, so I walked around the house with nothing but my robe on. The phone rang and the caller I.D. read that it was Denise.

"Hello," I said as my voice began to crack.

"I was just calling to see how you were doing. What have you been up to?"

"Nothing, I was just thinking about you."

"Do you need anything for the party?"

"All I need is you and your beautiful body." My compliment was intercepted by another call. "Hey, hold on for a minute. I have a beep. Hello?" I said as I clicked over to the other line.

"Hey baby, this is your mother. What are you doing? Did I catch you at a bad time baby?"

"No Ma. Hold on for a minute," I said as I clicked back over to Denise. "Hey Denise it's my mother. I'll call you tomorrow." I said as I ended my call with Denise. I then clicked back over to continue talking to my mother.

"Sorry about that. I'm back, Ma. Is everything ok?"

"Are you still going to pick me up from the airport tomorrow night?"

"What time does your flight get in?" I asked.

"I'm flying with United Air and my flight arrives in New York at eight thirty tomorrow night. Are you going to be there? You know I get lost in big airports."

"Yes, I'll be there. Have you heard from Tonya and Brian lately?"

"Yes I talked with her an hour ago. She and Brian will be at your house Friday morning. They are going to stay until Sunday night."

"That sounds good. I will be there at the airport tomorrow night. Call me before your plane leaves, okay?"

"Good night. I can't wait to see you."

"I can't wait either. Love you, Ma. Good night."

I could not believe that my mother was actually coming to visit me for a weekend. This would give us time to talk things through, and maybe do a little shopping. My mother was the queen of shopping. She could smell bargains from the parking lot. Before heading to bed, I went over to the window in my bedroom again as I seem to do every other night to steal a glance of my neighborhood. After minutes of watching nothing, I then looked upward into the sky and saw that it had no trace of any stars or a moon. I then realized that I was just like the night sky, dark and lonely. I walked away from the window and got into bed. On the right side of the bed were two more pillows. I reached over and grabbed both of them closer to me. As I cupped the pillows in my arms, I envisioned that the day would come when they were no longer the fillers of my agonizing pain.

Chapter 12

"Good morning, Dr. Phillips. This is Mr. Brown calling you from the Department of Children Services. We found a home for Jason Avery, and we have decided to release him from the hospital."

"That's wonderful. I can't believe that I'm actually hearing this." I said as I sat up against the mahogany finished wooden headboard connected to my bed. I was still asleep when Mr. Brown called me, but now I became fully awake.

"Have a good day, Dr. Phillips. Merry Christmas."

"You too, Mr. Brown."

I was ecstatic that Jason was finally able to have a family that would adopt him. With a lifted spirit and a joyful mood, I got the house ready for Tonya, Brian, and Mama's visit. It was going to be really great having my family at my house this year for Christmas. I saw this is as a time where healing could take place in my life, and closure to so many chapters can now finally close. After Tonya's wedding, and my confession to my mother I have made some progression. I will admit that the road to deliverance and a breakthrough has not been easy, but I had to keep the faith. Trials and tests I am told come to make you stronger, and I must say that my valley experiences have made me stronger. I am not sure if I am going to let my excessive consumption of liquor and wine go, but I have done quite well these past few days. I believe drinking is something that I inherited from my father. He would always drink away his pain and his problems. I once considered going to a support group, but my pride would not allow me. Pride can work for you and against you if one is not careful. I am probably in all the mess I'm in today because I allowed my pain to overtake me. I let a secret like dealing with my sexuality cause me to attempt suicide and depression. But like I said before, now I have faith, and I have hope that someday I can put all this behind me. For now, I have to take each day as it comes, and allow God to direct my path in life. After three hours of putting away clothes, cleaning the kitchen, cleaning the bathroom, and putting new sheets in the guest bedrooms, I decided I would sit down and relax and watch some television before I left to pick up my mother from the airport. Since I have been on vacation, I have not taken the time to just sit and do absolutely nothing. So I got comfy in my bed and then turned on the television to see what was current. That is when I heard the buzzer ring. When I went to the call box and asked who was there, I immediately knew it was Darren. The way I knew this is because I recognized his voice and I could hear him talking to someone. I hoped that it was not J.B. because if it were, I would not be able to deal with him. A few minutes later Darren appeared at my door, and to my discovery he was alone. I let out a sigh of relief after I realized Darren was alone.

"What a surprise. I didn't expect to see you so soon. What brings you by?" I asked.

"I remembered you said that you were on vacation this week so I decided to surprise you and come by."

"Cool man thanks for dropping by." I said.

"Why did you have this strange look on your face when you saw me at the door?" Darren asked as he walked to the kitchen in search of a bite to eat.

"Oh I just woke up. You know how it is man, when you are in a deep sleep and someone wakes you up." I lied.

"Yeah I know how that is. Where are the cookies and chips man?" Darren asked as he searched every cabinet for his prized possessions.

"You know I have started my workout with James, the trainer from

L.X. gym. He instructed me not to yield to temptation by storing food in my kitchen that would not help me attain my goal."

"So you really serious about this fitness thing, huh man?"

"I am trying to do something new in my life. I drink too much, and my day to day issues seem to be weighing me down. Therefore, I need a resort or an outlet to escape my issues and heal my pain."

"Speaking of healing, are you okay now? I mean you have been acting really strange these past couple of weeks. I know we talked before and I hope it is not the same thing you were dealing with a few months ago. I think you are hiding and withholding some valuable information from me. "

"No I have told you everything you need to know. I just need more time to cope with my private affairs that's all."

"Well I am here for you. You know that right?" Darren asked.

"Of course I do Darren. Well let's change the subject. How have things been going for you so far?" I asked Darren as he poured himself a glass of grape juice.

"It has been cool. I just got this little case I'm working on, but other than that I have been chilling."

"Yeah, I hear that man. I just wish I could take a break. You would think that being on vacation would be relaxing, but I have had so many personal things to do. But, after the holidays I will be able to at least have a few days to be alone and have a real vacation." I said.

"When Mama Phillips comes, I know you'll be able to relax. She is going to spoil you and do all of the cooking and cleaning."

"You are right about that. Moms still treats me like I'm her little boy when I'm around her. When I went home to Atlanta, she was fixing my shirt and telling me that I needed to wear a jacket. You know how she is."

"Jay, just be thankful that you still have your mother in your life. I would do anything to have my mother just spend the holidays with me man. Every since she died four years ago I still can't stop thinking about her."

"You are right. I guess I sometimes take her for granted. I know these past four years have been ruff for you, but hang in there. You are like family to me and I am here for you."

"Thanks for your support bro'. So, you have any plans for the rest of the day?" He asked as he wiped the tears from his eyes. I could see that he did not want me to see him in a vulnerable state of mind.

"Not really but I have been in the house all day. Perhaps I could go visit a few stores in Manhattan to pick up some possible gifts."

"That sounds like a plan to me Jay. I guess I will tag along with you because I would like to pick up a couple of gifts too."

I immediately got dressed, and Darren and I headed downtown to have a little brother to brother bonding time. I could think of no-one else in the world who knew me better than Darren. No matter what the problem, no matter how many times I had tried to cover of my mess, Darren was always there right by my side. Our friendship was one that was valued and I will always be grateful to God for that. Darren and I talked about his new girlfriend Pamela and he even said he invited her to come to church with us one Sunday so Denise and I could meet her. I asked if she would be at my annual Christmas party and he told me that she would not be in New York then. I told him that maybe we all could get together for New Year's and he told me he would keep me posted. The afternoon traffic was a little congested with commuters trying to make their way home or to their respective destinations. I was in no particular rush and I used this time to talk to Darren more. One hour later, Darren and I finally reached Manhattan and I then searched for a perfect parking spot. I eventually parked over on 34th Street so that Darren and I could walk around instead of driving.

I would have taken the train but driving into town and then parking seemed like the best thing to do. I really valued our brotherly bond and friendship. I am quite sure that if I would have told a few of my other male friends about what I was going through they would probably stop being friends with me. Darren was different, he was the brother I never had, and the friend I always needed, and for that I was grateful. Darren and I shopped mostly all afternoon and into the evening at many of the stores on 34th Street and even Fifth Avenue. We both then decided to stop later on that night at Bryant Park near Fifth Avenue to watch a few of the ice skaters in the park. Each year the park staff would hire a company to put together an ice skating ring. I had skated a few years ago in the park with Denise and Darren, and each of us had so much fun. I fell a few times, and Darren and Denise would help me up and then laugh at me at the same time. I will admit it was funny after the second and third time I fell. The first time I fell I was embarrassed so laughing was not my first response. Darren hanging out with me reminded me of how much fun I used to have. Here lately, I have been so serious and formal with Darren and even Denise.

I told Darren that I had to go and pick up my mother from the airport and I offered to take him back to his apartment. He took the train to my house, because from time to time he would ride public transportation instead of driving. Darren says that in order to be a real New Yorker, you needed to be out amongst the people. Darren and I grew up in the country, and I have always been proud of my country roots, but I think Darren wanted so much to fit in. I was always the leader and Darren was always the one trying to fit into a particular club or fraternity. The irony of it all is that he is now leading me and helping me to find my way in life. I left Darren's apartment in route to pick up my mother from the airport. Spending time with Darren allowed me to clear my thoughts and spend some time away from my condo. I also was very excited about my mother coming to visit me. When I got outside of the car pick up area for her flight, I spotted my mother right away. The way I was able to identify her is because she was the only one dressed like she was about to attend a prestigious award show. The attire she had on if you asked her would be her special occasion wear. I knew that she was proud to be my mother and I appreciated the fact she thought coming to see me was a special occasion.

"I am so glad to see you," I said as I kissed her on the left cheek and grabbed her carry on. She then told me that she had a lot of items with her, so when we arrived at the baggage claim, I rented a luggage cart. The heaviness of each suitcase felt as if she had large weights inside each bag. When I was a little boy, she would practically bring the whole house with her when we would go to Louisiana to see my grandmother. "She hasn't changed a bit," I thought as I placed the last bag on the cart.

"My God Jay you look like a stick. Why aren't you eating honey? And don't tell me different because I know you boy!" She suspiciously observed. The wedding hadn't been that long ago and she was acting as if she hadn't seen me in years. I did not feel I owed her any explanation so I did not respond. As I placed her bags in the trunk I tried to prepare myself to not to allow her to play the investigator role with me. So I thought that if I talked about my party and Tonya then at least I would be safe for a while.

"So what do you want to do first?" I said as I started the car.

"I want to go to bed darling. Mama is exhausted."

"I have your room all set up." I said.

"Oh I can't wait to see your place." She replied.

On the ride home my mother kept herself occupied with talking to me about different family members, and about how she loved Brian. I am surprised that Tonya has not told her yet about the baby, but I am sure when Tonya feels like telling her she would. Before going home I thought I would take my mother to a pizzeria, so that she could get a taste of some great New York pizza. She agreed to go and she even complimented on how delicious the pizza was in New York. She was also starting to act like an authentic tourist as she took a picture of everything she thought would be good for her scrap book. I did not mind, because this was the happiest I had seen my mother in quite some time. My goal was to make her enjoy herself, and from the looks of things it did not seem as if that was hard to do. I was able to get her to stay for two weeks, and I asked her to move here but she immediately declined. I have Darren and Denise here, but sometimes I wished my mother and sister were closer to me. But, my mother reminds me that she was born in the south and she was going to die in the south. In other words, there was no amount of persuasion that could change her mind. We finally reached my place and I enjoyed seeing the expression on my mothers face when we pulled up to my building. I got Carrington to carry her bags up and I then tipped him and wished him a good night. I told my mother to close her eyes and then when I opened the door to my condo she could open her eyes. I turned the key in the lock and then slowly opened the door.

"This is my place. What do you think?" I said as we walked inside.

"And there it is." She said with one of her famous sayings. "Look at this place, so warm and inviting. I love this son." She said as she continued to admire my art collection in the entertainment room. I continued the tour of my condo and then our last stop was to the guest bedroom where she would be sleeping in.

"This is the guest bedroom, where you'll be staying," I said as I placed her bags down on the floor next to the closet.

"Oh this room is nice. Do you have a private decorator? Or did you do it yourself?"

"I do everything myself. I get most of my ideas out of catalogs, and a few television shows I watch."

"I really like this and I am so, so proud of you." She said as she gave me a tight lemon squeeze hug.

For dinner, I warmed up some chicken and pasta I had made the night before, and I put some garlic rolls in the oven. My mother had to take over, so she found a can of corn in the cabinet above my kitchen sink and started cooking that to go along with the chicken and pasta. Then she made a salad and some tea. I told her to sit at the dining room table and I would serve her. One by one, I took the food out to the table. I poured us both some tea and sat down beside her.

"This tastes delicious," my mother said.

"Believe it or not, New York City supermarkets have some of the best prepared food departments," I said as I sipped my tea.

"Baby, how are you really doing?" She peered deeply into my eyes in that "Mama knows you" way. She could tell that something still wasn't right with me, but she failed at getting a confession.

"I'm doing fine." I answered her. "I've just been burning it at both ends trying to get ready for the party, for the visit, and for Tonya and Brian's arrival. Ah, it's so good to have family at my place this Christmas. It really makes this place seem like a home.

"Mama sure has been keeping you in prayer. I know that the Lord is going to give you full deliverance and heal you."

"Thanks, Ma." I sighed. I was temporarily safe. Once again, I was able to mask my true feelings. "That should hold her for a while," I thought. But I have to be careful not to let my depression run rampant, especially when Tanya arrived. She and Ma worked like a tag-team, and were masters at reading my actions. I had to remember to keep moving, keep busy, because a moving target is hard to hit. I know if either one of them sensed the slightest bit of apprehension on me, they would circle me like vultures just waiting for the right moment to pounce. They always meant well, but this was something that neither one had the power to fix. This one was all on me.

"I see the way you looked at me when I asked you if you were doing okay. A mother knows when her son is faking. She knows when he has it all together and when he is totally not together."

"I'm just so glad you're here." I said with genuine sincerity.

"We have all weekend to talk about anything you want to. But right now, Mama Diva has to get some rest." She said as she went into the guest bedroom.

"Rest up then. This is going to be an exciting holiday." I said as I followed her to her room.

"Goodnight," my mother said, as she gracefully positioned me to the door. I took the hint and more so the opportunity to escape any deep probing conversation and perform my usual "in for the evening" rituals before heading to bed.

I went back into the kitchen, and cleared off the table, and then I did the dishes. Later on I went back to see how my mother was settling in. I stopped right outside the bedroom and noticed her making her final descent to bed.

"Can I ask you a question before you go to bed?" I asked from her doorway. She was standing by the nightstand, taking off her jewelry.

"Yes, what is it son?"

"Do you ever get lonely in that big house you live in? I mean do you ever pray that God would send you someone?" She took a moment and looked at me while she made up her mind whether to open up, or just deflect the question with a clichéd response.

"Sit here for a minute," she said as she rested her right hand on the bed for me to sit next to her.

"After your father walked out on us, I felt as though the best thing that I ever had was gone. But you know what? Your father was not the best thing I had. My children and God were the best things I have. I don't know exactly what it is you're going through now but whatever it is, pray. God answers prayers and he is standing nigh."

"You're right. I just feel so alone here by myself every night," I said as I put my head on my mothers shoulder.

"Are you and that boy still, you know?" She asked uncomfortably.

"Right now I don't want to get into that. But what I will say is that he is out of my life for now. I just want somebody to love me. I have the Lord on my side comforting me every time I'm feeling low. But Ma, I need a physical person. I'm sorry that I brought this up. Get some rest Ma. I will see you in the morning."

"I love you son, I really do. You just listen to what Mama has said. Pray, okay darling? I love you, and I'm here for you. If you want me to stay longer, I will. Just tell me what I can do to help you be happy. I will do the best that I can while I'm here."

"I really appreciate that, and I know you love me. See you in the morning, and thanks for the chat."

"Good night. And don't let any of this get the best of you. It all will pass away in due time. Just have faith and believe."

"Thanks for everything." I said as I gently closed the door. I have been fortunate enough to have a caring, loving, and understanding mother. I have wonderful friends and family that I know that I can rely on, no matter what. Nothing that I have gone through has been easy to deal with, but I am still here. I have to take life one day at a time, and let tomorrow work for its self. Tonight I was not going to bed defeated, nor was I going to shed another tear. Tonight I was going to go to bed with a clear mind and anticipate seeing my sister and her husband tomorrow. A change has come over me and I don't plan on turning back now.

Chapter 13

I WAS AWAKENED BY MY mother's singing and the clunking sounds of pots. The clock on the wall next to my stove read 2:00 P.M. I had slept all morning and almost part of the afternoon.

"Boy you scared me! Come on and sit down here. The food will be ready in a few minutes." She said.

"Food smells good. What's on the menu?" I asked.

"Mama's cooking a little bit of everything. Some French toast, scrambled eggs, blueberry muffins, bacon, and to top it off, some good old fashioned grits. I thought I would fix you breakfast since that seems to be the only food you have in here. That would probably explain this sudden weight loss of yours. But I am not going to go there with you right now."

"That sounds good. You're going to have to visit me more often," I said as I opened up the newspaper. I still did not comment on her pressing remarks, again I did not want to talk about anything personal with her right now.

I reviewed the newspaper and read an article about a man close to where I lived who got shot last night at the drug store a few blocks away from my house. I really hated to read reports in the newspapers about brothers dying or getting gunned down.

"What are you reading?" My mother asked as she rinsed her hands in the sink.

"Some brother got shot last night at a local convenience store. I'm just reading what happens almost every day in New York."

"How do you cope with living here? Atlanta is big, but the crime rate is not as massive as it is here in New York."

"I can take care of myself. I mind my own business, and I have God. And crime is crime no matter where you live."

"I guess you're right, but you living up here scares me. You probably haven't had a decent meal in God knows when. Where are your plates?"

"In the cabinet on the right," I said as I folded up my newspaper.

"These are very nice. I love the animal print on the plates. I might have to take these home with me."

"Those plates you can have. I don't know why I bought them in the first place. It's not like I'm ever home to make use of them anyway."

The food was good and I ate my weight in bacon. My mother insisted that she do the dishes, and for me to get ready for tonight. I told her I had a dishwasher, but she of course insisted on doing it by hand. I finished eating my last piece of toast and then my mother and I prepared for Tonya and Brian's arrival. This is their first time in New York. And the only reason that they knew how to get to my condo is because I ordered them car service and instructed the driver where to drop them off. I informed Tonya of what she should look for when she went to the pickup area. I told Tonya to look for the guy with the sign that read "Dr. Jackson Phillips' Party."

My mother and I cleared the middle of the entertainment room so we could make way for the tree. This was the first year that I decided to order a real live white pine tree. I liked the look better than those plastic ones I had growing up. Before I could even get the ornaments out the box, the doorbell rang. It was the delivery guy with my tree. When I opened the door there was a slender Italian guy with my tree on a dolly at my front door. It really was a sight to behold, and I was going to have a ball decorating it. After about five minutes, I heard a knock at the door. With a wide grin and warm embraces, I invited my sister and her husband inside my home. My sister and her husband looked like a match made in heaven, and I could really see that she was completely happy with him. They had arrived sooner than I expected, but the fact that they landed safely was good enough for me. It was like click, flash, and pow. Everything happened so quickly. It seems as though I had just woken up and before I knew it everything since breakfast was full speed ahead.

"This is a nice place you have here, Jay." Tonya said as she scanned the entertainment room.

"Thanks, Tonya. I am so glad to see you, I really am."

"Same here, Jay. Same here." She said as she gave me a real tight hug.

My mother and Tonya went off to the other guest bedroom to get Tonya settled in as Brian and I setup for the party. We moved a few tables, and cleared the bar for Darren. He was going to be my bartender tonight, and I had given him a list of what to stock the bar with tonight. Tonya and my mother decorated the place with the poinsettias I had bought earlier and fresh beige table cloths for the tables.

Five o' clock arrived faster than I anticipated, but everything was just about ready. Tonya and Brain were in the guest room getting ready and Ma went back in her room to put on her final touches. She believed divas didn't just arrive at functions they made an "entrance." Even though it technically wasn't her party, she knew the floor would belong to her upon her descent into the party. And so she continued to prepare until her cue.

The hurriedness of the day kept my inner turmoil at bay as I began to adjust to the holiday spirit. I was glad that I didn't cancel the party, as there were many sleepless nights I spent pondering, should I just call it off? Denise would not be there and that strange reality left a hole deeper than any Christmas carol or tinseled store bought tree could ever fill. But Mama, Tonya, and even Brian had been looking forward to the trip and I couldn't selfishly disappoint them. Besides everyone who knew of me, would suspect that something was suspiciously wrong being that my party has been a time honored tradition since my first year in New York.

The doorbell rang just in time to snap me back to reality. The rumaki was sizzling in the broiler almost making a fast descent to charcoal heaven if I didn't remove it immediately. I made it to the door as the bell began to chime its second series of two long and short buzzes. Sheila arrived with a gentleman friend and some of my church-folk followed her promenade.

"Rob, this is Dr. Phillips. Dr. Phillips this is Rob...Robert Lewis. He's a paralegal for Tyson, Brevard, and Davis." Sheila beamed.

She carried an aura about her that I never noticed before. She boasted a confidence that didn't put on arrogance, but continued genuine warmth and sincerity. I greeted Sheila's friend with the standard hand shake and welcomed him to the party. I took Sheila's hand and gently pulled her closer to me, while grazing her blushing cheek with my lips. I whispered deliberately, "Alright now Miss Thing!" Sheila walked over sheepishly and then took Robert by the arm.

"Dr. Phillips, your place looks great! It looks like you really knocked yourself out these past few days." Sheila exclaimed.

"I see I am not the only one knocked out!" My glance fell on Robert, who never noticed anything but Sheila.

Sheila blushed a radiant rose red and released a coy chuckle.

"You really look radiant! I'm so glad you came!" I commented releasing her from her moment of awkwardness.

"I know! I can't stop looking at her." Robert confided. Sheila found herself back at the center of awkwardness and decided to rescue herself. She looked at Robert and offered to help him find the bar.

"Just help yourself Rob. One of my frat brothers is suppose to come and bartend for me. But you don't have to wait for him." I suggested. I gave Sheila a wink as she sauntered with Rob to the bar. There was a twang of relief in seeing her with Robert. Sheila deserved someone decent and he looked like he would spend a lot of time trying to make her happy.

The room swelled with more guests, and Tonya and Brian had finally joined the party. After a few cordial introductions, I released them on their own recognizance and left them mingling. The next few doorbell rings could barely be heard as the condo soon reached its limit of small talk and chit chat. The music crept its way past the background noise and commanded direct and full attention from anyone who could keep a beat or even those who thought they could. The party was in full swing. The Diva, Ms. Phillips, set her entrance to Whitney Houston's rendition of "Joy to the World" as she walked into the party in grand style. She towered with perfect southern grace as she skillfully steeped purposely through the crowd in her fierce Jimmy Choo strapped heels. If there was anyone in the room that missed the proper introduction from me, Ma took it upon herself to do the honors. And what an honor it was as she extended her right hand forward with an ever so slight dip in the wrist as she carefully enunciated her title, "Ms. Phillips, Jackson's mother. It's a pleasure to meet you as well."

Darren arrived complete with apologies for being late. After a quick check-in he took his place behind the bar. I managed to slip behind the bar and shouted in his ear, "Any word from her?" I asked hopefully.

"She said she might. It just depended on how she was feeling after work. But this is Denise we are talking about. You know what might means man."

Darren continued his labor and his friendly banter as he served up the usual party favorites, soft drinks of any variety, a little wine with a few sprits here and there, all with the absence of any significant amount of alcohol. This was a mixed crowd and there were some who soberly and deliberately denounced its presence in the name of Jesus. Nevertheless, the hard stuff had been clearly stashed by yours truly. In parties past, the church people usually tired out first always leaving the rest of the night up for the true party people. My parties had become legendary; often ending with a polite scrambled egg breakfast served the next morning for revelers who had their car keys removed from their possession the night before.

This year was different though. I mean my sister and her husband were here and of course my mother. Its not that any of them had a problem with alcohol or those who consumed, it just wasn't that kind of party. This party was different. Everyone seemed to be having a good time, but as for me I was just going through the motions. Denise had her reasons for not coming I suppose. It's like she and I broke up twice, once as an engaged couple, then as friends. We've spoken a little since I revealed my confession, but there was a definite strain. I could sense that she was trying to understand but yet felt conflicted with her own feelings. At this point I could only speculate what she must be thinking, but soon revoked my right to do that. "If she wants to talk," I rationalized, "She'll find a way to speak her mind." At any rate I worked the crowd in between replenishing food trays, removing abandoned cups, and joining the impromptu "Cha-Cha-Slide" that inevitably invaded any party where two or more were gathered. The doorbell stopped ringing as the door turned into a revolving door as people entered and exited at will. The music thumped instructions and we all dutifully obeyed while each of us tried to make the calculated steps of our own. "Criss-cross, criss-cross, left foot stomp, right foot."

My perfect Cha-Cha came to a sudden and complete stop as I looked up from the floor and noticed the front door. I abandoned the Cha-Cha slide groupies, and made a dash to the door. My heart moved much more rapidly then it did its own dance. As a matter of fact it fluttered. The feeling threw me for a second in that it was a sensation not felt for along time passing. Denise hesitated, but for a second trying to take the crowd in all at once.

She squinted as she searched for a familiar face. Her search ended as I finally made my way over to her and her anxiety soon turned into soothing relief as she flashed me one of her smiles.

"Wow Jay! Look at this place," she had to shout over the crowd. "It looks amazing! I'm so sorry I hadn't confirmed much earlier that I would be attending tonight." She said in a regretful tone.

My spirits took a giant leap over the inner depression that I managed to suppress up until now. My first instinct was to grab her by the arm and whisk here away from everyone. But I managed to contain my instinct and greeted her with my usual hug and peck on the cheek. She looked alluring, revealing enough of her sensuality to make her honorably desirable. She most definitely was not dressed for Sunday morning service, but the side split never restricted her legs stride as she moved towards me. The dress she was wearing knew exactly what to do, hugging her hips with just enough pressure while releasing a flow of silky soft landings just above the knee. I received her hand and spun her in a slow purposeful circle, giving her the moment to show her God given talent.

"One of your creations, no doubt." I finally replied.

"So you like the dress Jay?"

"Yes I do. Yes, I, I really do." I stammered shamefully. My voice trailed off and I was now smiling uncontrollably. Something was different, very different about tonight. Denise not only radiated the room but she struck something so deep inside of me. I began a slow and private shake, the kind you set when that secret high school crush you had says a friendly hello. She broke my trance when she inquired, "Where is your mother? I've been waiting to see her here tonight."

"The Queen is working." I countered.

"Working?" She exclaimed.

"Yes, working the party. She is gracing us with her southern genteel-divaness. Miss Scarlet does not have a damn thing on my mother, Denise."

Denise took the joke with her usual friendly finesse and assured me she would find her. I leaned in real close before releasing her hand to let her know that I really needed to talk to her privately. Her spontaneous gaze let her acknowledge my eagerness without offering a reply. Another benefit from a close friendship, the use of the unspoken radar to communicate making words unnecessary.

"I will meet you in the kitchen in five minutes," she offered."

"Sounds good," I confirmed.

Resisting the urge to run through the crowd, I continued to mingle my way through the revelers until I reached the bar area. Although still going very strong, the D.J. gave cue for a mellowed out mood as guests settled into ultimate huddles of conversations. The dance floor gave way to the steppers in the crowd who were not shy about showing off their smoothly choreographed moves. I felt reassured that everyone was having a good time and would not need me these next few minutes. When I turned around Denise was right behind me with a smirk on her face. Without hesitation I whisked her off to the kitchen.

"I'd been wanting to talk to you so much since that day we had lunch, but didn't want to impose on your space. I felt you needed some time to gain perspective about some things. I also was afraid of you deciding not to be in my life anymore. I guess I felt the longer I took to confront you then you would be around that much longer."

I finally found the nerve to give her a real opportunity to open up to me and tell me what she thought of me as a person. I was ready to hear whatever emotions I had coming to me for whatever I put her through. I felt I owed her at least that even if it meant our friendship would end.

"You hurt me Jay," she began truthfully. "Not because you were dealing with your issues, but because somehow you didn't trust me with the truth. All relationships whether their family, love, or platonic friendships, all relationships are built on a foundation of trust. I felt insulted that after all that we have gone through, all I thought I meant to you, you didn't trust me. So I was angry! So much so I couldn't go to Tonya's wedding with you."

"So what brought you here tonight? We haven't spoken much since lunch that day. I really didn't think you'd show up Denise."

"It's called forgiveness, Jay. I first had to forgive myself for being so blindly in love that I didn't see the signs. My forgiveness of me left me with a lot of animosity and anger toward you and I knew in order to be emotionally healthy, I had to forgive you. So I prayed, and prayed and didn't stop until I walked in my closet just a few hours ago and picked out this dress to come here. I had let it all go and made a choice to accept your choice and that is to move on." Her confidence never took a back seat to her compassion and my heart ached for her the more she talked.

"Denise I never wanted to hurt you! I've been hiding behind this mask for so long, I thought I'd never be able to remove it. It's so hard for me to understand all of this, let alone expecting you to understand it. I can't even say for sure what is going to go on with me. I go through the motions everyday, like going to work day to day to just help people just like me. But behind my own door, I can't even help myself. I want so badly for this torment to end. And I keep asking God for a sign of deliverance. But I just don't see it. I don't know what His design is or what He is telling me." My words flowed with a subtle ease that I found ironically therapeutic. But in an instant, the comfort was gone. Denise and I were no longer the only two people in the kitchen.

"You want deliverance? From what? Or from whom I should say? From me? Or from finally admitting what you truly are!"

Denise and I both froze in our stance as J.B. entered the kitchen and the conversation.

"What the hell are you doing here?" I demanded. I hadn't sent him an invitation, but the word did get out about the party, so it was no secret.

"Look Jay, I can't stay for this. I guess I'm just not there yet. You go do what you do best. Maybe I shouldn't have come, but like I said I'm moving on." Denise protested.

"Yeah perhaps you should move on!" J.B. screamed.

Denise hesitated before angrily storming out of the room. "Father-Jesus help the Christian woman in my soul! This brother does not want to go there with me!" She shouted as she left my condo.

J.B. attempted to say something but his ill remark hardly made it past the doorway. The music was too loud and Denise was gone.

"You need to leave my house now J.B., right now. Why are you here?" I asked.

"I just wanted to see you, to talk to you. To talk some sense into you man. You wouldn't talk to me on the phone," J.B. pleaded.

"This is not the time, nor the place for you to pour out your feelings. My mother, my family, and even my friends are here. This is a big mistake for you to come here and do this."

J.B. stepped toward me with a determination I'd never seen in him before. He was relentless and set on making a statement, a horrifying statement that would leave me exposed to anyone and everyone within earshot. Though he and I were the only ones present in the kitchen, this had all the ear markings of a nasty confrontation. At that point I tried to calm myself so as to stay in control of the situation. It was a futile attempt.

"Jay, you can't run from me and you can't hide either. You think you can just pray your way out of this one? Well you can't, I am not going anywhere."

J.B.'s words hit me like a ton of bricks. How could he stand there and mock my faith in that way. At that moment I felt anger that was being driven by passion I thought I once felt for him. In an instant, those feelings turned to shame and disgust. Everything I tried to suppress came hurling to the surface no longer waiting to be released. The time had come and I was ready to give into it.

"Hold up! You have no right to come into my home with these asinine accusations. First of all, you don't know me. You freely gave up that right in college at *Terminus* when you were playing the hot-shot basketball star that couldn't risk his reputation being seen with me. And now you come up in here after all of this time with some half-cocked notion that you and I could have a life together. Well, you're a day late and a dollar short. There is no us, we have no future together, so you might as well go back to where you came from." J.B. grabbed me suddenly and jerked me close to him so that we stood eye to eye. "Look me in the eye's." He challenged. "And tell me you are being honest. Go ahead!" He screamed louder. I stood there stunned at his abruptness. His grip remained tight on my shoulders as he continued to taunt me. "You can't can you? But yet you continue this pathetic life, while you think you have everyone fooled. But what happens to you every night Jay? What happens when you find yourself in this big empty place alone? You invite these people to come and see you living large and doing well being the great doctor that can fix everyone else except himself. Jay at night you crawl in bed and then the loneliness starts to swallow you whole. What do you do then? Let me guess, what you pray? But as soon as you get up off your knees you think about calling me."

At that moment my stance was no longer frozen and I broke free from J.B.'s grip while my hand found its way to his neck. In one single death grip, I pushed him violently against the stove yet never releasing my hand from his neck. The crash sent people running to see what was going on, and I could see Darren leading the way. He found me with my hand still clutching J.B. by the throat as he choked helplessly under my grip. My rage consumed me so rapidly that I never had a chance to think. It continued to travel through my body that I was no longer conscious of my actions. Darren stepped in quickly and tried to pry my fingers away from J.B.'s throat. "Jay, man what are you doing? Let him go! Whatever this is it's not worth you going to jail for man. Let him go Jackson." Darren begged me. Darren's plea finally broke the trance I had been in for a while. I regained control, but I continued to curse profusely at J.B. until he finally left. He was horrified and stormed out of the party spewing a few obscenities of his own. The party broke up as everyone took the cue from J.B. and began to leave. Tonya and Brian stepped in as host and hostess and saw everyone out. I was an emotional mess. Darren tried to talk to me but he had little success. I stayed in my home office because I needed sometime to regroup. Darren attempted to talk to me, but I wouldn't surrender anything remotely useful, so he eventually gave up and assured me he would stop by tomorrow so we could talk.

Everybody retired to their respective corners while I remained silent and unreachable. I was in no mood for recanting what happened between J.B. and Denise for that matter. The flames of rage and furry

114

burned incessantly, and I finally exited my bedroom in search of the bottle of Scotch I put away in the cabinet over the refrigerator. The party was over and I was tired. I was tired of hiding, tired or pretending, tired of lying to myself, and tired of betraying my faith in God. I let the bottle of Scotch comfort me to a slow and quiet stupor of shame and self pity.

Chapter 14

"JAY, WAKE UP! IT'S ALMOST noon! Get up! The phone has been ringing off the hook. Do you hear me? Get up now boy!" Tonya's pleading was desperate, but I didn't care. I just wanted to sleep. The Scotch wore off way to soon and left a massive headache as its calling card. Tonya's voice became a series of unnerving shrills that had the same effect on me as someone scratching their fingernails across a chalk board. Eventually I threw in the white towel and surrendered to her beckoning.

"Alright! Stop the screaming, I'm getting up." I made the terrible mistake of shouting at her and my head quickly reminded me of the night before.

"Hurt don't it? Humph serves you right. I made you some coffee in the kitchen go on and get some before it gets cold." My mother said.

"Oh Ma! I…I didn't see you there. Good morning." I attempted to approach her with a kiss but she waved me off.

"Uh huh! Don't come near me with that morning breath. And now that I think of it, the morning has passed you by son. You slept right through most of the day. I guess you think someone is going to just stop their day because you decide you want to wake up late. Well you can think again. Now go and get your coffee, and I placed some Tylenol on the counter for you as well to help that headache of yours."

She continued to mutter as I stumbled my way to the kitchen.

"I don't see how people can come to your house and cause problems like that boy did last night. Where is Jesus in all of this? I did not know you had all of this going on. I knew you had been hiding a lot from me, but I would never have imagined this. And to think that you had gotten over all of this. Prayer is the answer." My mother went on and on as she worked her way throughout my condo.

I eventually blocked out her complaining and settled my mind on other things. I gulped the coffee and made my way to my bathroom in my bedroom to take a shower. My words were few, and while no one seemed to be up for any kind of confrontation, nobody seemed to mind my pensive mood. As I headed upstairs my eye caught the glistening package that stood apart from the rest of the gifts underneath the tree. It was the biggest one and commanded a lot of curiosity, as everyone fantasized that the box was surely meant for them. My hesitation ticked by for a few seconds as I recalled that I had planned to see Jason Avery today. It was not the usual protocol to visit one of my clients in their home, but I promised to be more than just a therapist to him. Today however, with the present state of things, my plans changed. I rationalized that as long as I brought him a present, he wouldn't care whether he got it on Christmas morning or the day after. His fascination with trains led me to a hobby shop in New Jersey in search of a H.O. Scale model train set complete with an engine. It would be good for him to have a hobby. And I thought I could continue to cultivate his interest in trains with trips to the hobby shop every now and then. This way I could get him some add on pieces to his set. I dismissed the thought, and conceded that I would visit him another day, perhaps tomorrow.

After I showered, I hurriedly got dressed and left the condo without much of a word to anyone. I set out for destinations unknown feeling like I had to run. My cell phone rang continuously until I finally turned it off with each call going unanswered. "Drive," I repeated out loud. "Just drive." My mind raced faster than the car so much so that I could barely keep up. The thoughts were heard yet fleeting as it appeared that almost everyone I knew crossed my muddled up mind. My mother and our past together, my father and his absence from my life, that bastard that robbed me of my innocence as a young boy, J.B. and his words still stinging my ears, and the reality of my life caught in sin and despair. I stopped suddenly oblivious to where I was going. The road was sparse with traveler's which perpetuated my feelings of loneliness. I lowered my head, resting face down on the steering wheel as my body began a slow intense quiver. My body shook as the tears blinded my sight. The sobs turned into wails as I boldly confronted God with my doubtful questions. The air stifled me and I felt breathless. I wrestled with the seatbelt until it finally released its hold on me. I flung my body to the ground in one helpless motion landing on my knees. My face turned upward towards the sky as I demanded God to hear me.

My words were captured by my bitterness and would only sound like the desperate cry of a mad man. I was alone and forsaken and I confronted God face on. I went back and forth with the words forsaking honor for self pity. I didn't thank God. Instead I chastised Him for not making me the man I wanted to be. I criticized His will as being punitive and judgmental. I rejected His mercy and demanded full restitution for all the pain I had suffered during my life. I was beyond bitter, and I wanted to give into my own weakness. By the time I got up off my knees, I was drained of all my energy. My legs wobbled from the weight of my body, and began to buckle under me. I steadied myself, leaning on the roof of the car, when I noticed the entire car was wet. As I looked down at myself so were my clothes. My knees were muddy as bits of finely ground gravel clung to my pants. It had rained. I was soaking wet, yet I never felt a drop. Nor could I account to how much time I had spent out there either. I realized that dusk was just settling in over the horizon, and then I could finally feel the falling temperatures as the wind swept across my face. I felt a small measure of relief though without a resolved resolution. As far as I knew J.B. was still running around out there like a loose cannon ready to fire on me at anytime. My family is probably worried sick about me right about now, and Denise may never ever want to have anything to do with me. The way things looked to her when J.B. came on the scene at the party must have embarrassed her. My heart ached at the thought of her standing there not knowing what she was caught up in. She had been the most innocent in all of this. From day one, she never knew what was going on with me. And for her to be degraded in the home that she always felt welcomed in had to be devastating.

"She'll never forgive me," I admitted out loud. And quite frankly I wasn't up to asking her to. I had done enough damage to this woman. I should just disappear from her existence. You know, let her find the rich full and happy life she deserved without the likes of me screwing it up. I had been driving so long until I had no idea where I was. I let the highway lead me back to familiar surroundings, and I soon found myself taking the exit that would lead me to my office. I needed to take refuge in that I wasn't ready to face my family just yet. The thought of a place where I would go and not have to answer any questions or give an account as to my whereabouts for the last six hours, motivated me to speed up. I stopped my car in front of the liquor store right across the street from my office to seek the services the bottle of Chivas Regal Scotch would soon provide for me.

I enjoyed the taste of wine, and challenged myself to learn more about the art of fine wine. But ironically it had been J.B. that introduced me to Scotch. Even though I rarely drank it for any occasions, I always kept a bottle stored in my house. I laughed to myself at the irony as I grabbed the brown paper bag with the Scotch by the neck. It would serve as the sacrificial lamb to my worship of self pity, as I exited the store without uttering a word. The night security officer greeted me with the standard salutation, and took liberties to offer extended conversation.

"Good evening Dr. Phillips. It's crazy to see you here this time of night. Usually you're headed out right about now instead of coming in," he laughed.

I passed on the opportunity to give him a response, and I let my gaze blaze a searing hole in his eyes, sending a clear message that I was not to his standard blue collar banter. I continued past him and made my way straight to the elevator. It was a quick ride to my floor in that the building was virtually unoccupied. It was peculiar in a way, that I would find myself here in the office seeking a place of refuge in my own environment. My clients come here for refuge from their environments, while trying to gain perspective on their problems. It's funny, because I'm the one they come to with their issues. I laughed out loud acknowledging the irony as I announce, "The Doctor is in!"

The daybed is a welcoming sight as I continue to chuckle at the sarcasm of it all. I let the Scotch out of the bag, and poured a long swallow down my throat, as I nestled against the pillows. "I'm the Doctor, damn it! I'm the damn Doctor and I should know better," I shouted to the empty chair. I continued to take swigs from the bottle as I contemplated how to play the roles of both patient and doctor. "This is where I fix things! But I can't fix this!" I declared to the emptiness of the room.

I stumbled to my desk and then I decided to check the messages. I hadn't bothered to turn my cell phone on, and I knew by now that my family was probably questioning my whereabouts. Darren was more than likely dragged into hunting me down, as my mother was a relentless woman, and would insist that he help her find me. Everyone would more than likely be worried with the exception of Denise. I lost my balance as I walked in the dark reaching for the chair behind the desk and fell in it.

The message signal blinked incessantly casting an evil red glow across the desk. I fought hard to focus on the keypad as my eyes blurred together any images that looked like numbers. The Scotch was doing its job as the mellowness of the elixir tickled me. I laughed at the absurdity of not being able to focus on the keypad and clumsily reached for the desk lamp. My attempt failed miserably as the lamp retreated from my grasp and hurled itself over the edge of the desk. My laughter was incessant as I scrambled to the floor. I crawled on my hands and knees vowing to rescue my poor lamp from the impeding destruction it was headed for. I tried to return it to its proper place from where I was kneeling on the floor, but could not get my vision to cooperate. My legs became instant allies with the Scotch and would not stand upright. I surrendered myself to the floor in front of the desk, and let my fingers explore the keypad on the telephone without assistance of my eyes.

It seemed like an eternity to find the right buttons, but I finally found the speaker and the playback buttons. I felt arrogantly victorious and settled on the floor with my back pressed against the desk. I listened to the messages without a slightest bit of concern for the pleading voices begging for me to call them back. The machine retrieved a message without words. The background sounds were the familiar muttering of muddled bantering and voices demanding to be heard. But no one voice took the lead to reveal the nature of the call. The noises ended without a clue as to who the messenger was. The bottle sat obediently between my legs as I threw down swallows from time to time after I checked another message. I felt a nod and a swag of my head as the Scotch advanced my body. Sometimes when a major catastrophe occurs, people relate the event to the smallest of details leading up to the disaster. For instance, the name of any song playing on the radio moments before a horrible car accident. Or the asymmetrical pattern of the wallpaper in the bedroom, when an unfaithful lover's caught in the act.

The next message was such a detail. My usual attention to my messages was arrested by the effects of the alcohol, and I found it difficult to pay close attention. But reality snatched me up, slapped me repeatedly across the face, and finally knocked me on my ass.

"Dr. Phillips? Dr. Phillips this is Jason's case manager. I was hoping by some odd chance you were in your office. I've been trying to reach you all afternoon on your office and cell phone. This call is about Jason, something has happened and I need you to contact me right away. Right now I am at St. John's Children's Hospital, there has been a terrible accident involving Jason, the detail of which I'll update you on when you call me back."

Click...the phone went dead and the office returned to its silence. The news had a major effect in that I was to try and regain control as soon as possible. I searched through the database of phone numbers that Sheila kept on her computer at her desk in the reception area. After skimming through hundreds of phone numbers, I was able to locate the case manager's number. On the message he did not leave his number, assuming I already knew it. The phone rang only once and he picked up the phone. When he realized who I was, he went into all the details about Jason and the accident. He assured me that he would call me and give an update on what would happen next. I became very distraught as I tried to make my way back to my office. I managed to make my way back inside my office, and I dashed right back in the chair behind my desk. How did I let this happen? What kind of mentor was I? Jason needed me, not as a professional doctor, but as a friend, and I wasn't there for him.

I had given him my card with my cell number written on the back. I told him that card was just for him only and to use it whenever he really needed to talk to me. The thought jolted me from the chair as I raced across the room looking for my jacket. My cell phone was still in my pocket conveniently turned off. The concern and disgust I felt sent the phone hurling through the air across the room landing with a hard crash against the wall. The pieces scattered as I fell to my knees and wept uncontrollably. Jason had been anxious about the new family and promised me he would give the "Richardson's" a fair chance. I told him that Christmas time was the perfect time for giving, and that he could give me the gift of giving his new family a chance. He told me that no one has ever given him anything on Christmas, but said he would try and get along with everyone. Our conversation ended with my promise to visit him on Christmas day with a very special present.

At last thought, the present was still laying patiently under the tree. For some reason it didn't beckon my command for immediate delivery and I felt quite at ease ignoring it. I selfishly took the privilege of an innocent child's trust and cast it aside as an unimportant obligation. Jason had been let down again by another adult offering him promises. And while he was lying in a hospital bed, the present remained underneath my Christmas tree.

Chapter 15

I FINALLY PICKED UP THE phone and dialed my condo. It was answered on the first ring. I knew there would be a lot of questions about where I was and what I was doing. I decided to reject any questions about anything. Right now I had to have answers about Jason. Somehow I was able to fight through my mother's concerns, and constant yelling to really get to the premise of what had taken place. She found out through Jason's new family that Jason had become out of control when I didn't keep my word about coming to see him. It seems that Jason had tried to call me at my house and on my cell phone. He became belligerent and defiant when any attempts to console him were made. Apparently he ran out the house with everyone chasing behind him, in hopes of getting him to calm down. Mr. Richardson finally caught up with Jason, but he struggled with Mr. Richardson until he finally broke loose. He ran out into the street without looking and was hit by a car. The car hit him pretty hard, placing him in a coma with internal injuries.

"Jay! Jay! Say something!" My mother demanded."Jay, are you still there?"

I broke my silence briefly, "Yeah, Ma," my voice cracked.

"Jay, I know you probably feel bad right now, but you know that

Jason had problems long before now son. It's not your fault..." her voice trailed off and ended when I put the receiver back on the cradle on my desk.

I stood up and walked over to the bookshelf behind my desk. I felt all at once helpless yet humble to my true self. Something was happening that I could not explain. All of a sudden I wanted to go back and try and find the beginning of all of this. Maybe I could put some real meaning to all of it, and perhaps I could find out just when these feelings started. But how far back do I need to go? What would digging up my past do to help me now? How did I get to this point?

My eyes fell upon a familiar object sitting pushed out from all the other books. As I drew closer to make out what the book was I realized as I read the side title that it was my college yearbook. I thumbed through the pages and then reminisced amongst the once familiar faces where names slowly disappeared from my memory between the elapsed time since the last time I looked at the book.

I lingered a long time at the picture of Denise and I sitting in the gazebo outside the dorm quad. It was a popular spot for the couples to get together in that it had its own built in romance. You could consider yourself lucky to find it empty at any given time in that most couples jumped at the chance for a spot when they could get a chance to be alone. My dorm-mate Kevin lived next door to me and was a photographer for the yearbook staff. One day Denise and I were lucky enough to grab a spot under the gazebo, and Kevin seized the opportunity to get a candid shot of us sitting together.

We were discussing our future together and the gaze in our eyes held so much hope for a happy future together. Kevin's photographic genius captured the moment with such realistic intensity; the editor picked it to appear in the yearbook. The picture always made me smile, and one even cracked through surpassing the pain, the guilt, and the Scotch for just a second. I threw back the last swallow and let the empty bottle fall to the end of the desk until it eventually fell to the ground sending an empty whistle sound. Pieces shattered but I was totally unaffected. The page jumping led me to the pages that glorified the school's athletic achievements for the year. It had been a stellar season for the basketball team. J.B. had been instrumental in landing the team to a conference victory. It had been a first for *Terminus University* and the yearbook staff had chronicled the season in pictures with full spreads that went on for pages end. I flipped through some more pages at a frantic pace trying to get past all of the pictures with J.B.'s face, J.B.'s seasonal statistics, J.B. and the coach, J.B. and the M.E.A.C. trophy the team won.

My hands trembled at the turning of each page. Suddenly my mind went through a whirl wind as the memories of faces flashed at lighting speed in my head. I blinked repeatedly but the images remained. I rose from my desk and began to look all around the office trying desperately to focus on something else. But all I could see were the images from my past. It was as if every negative experience permeated the room and held me hostage in my own mess. Denise's face when I broke up with her, J.B.'s blank expressions when he tried to cover up the fact that he never knew me when we were in college, my mother running away from me in terror when I told her my dilemma, Jason's tear strained face when I didn't show up, and the lifeless expression of a comatose little boy lying in a hospital bed without faith and hope.

I tried to scream, but nothing would come out. The faces were drawing closer to me, and I began to swing wildly at the air trying to make them go away. I yelled out to God but the harder I tried to yell all that came out was hot stale breath left behind by the Scotch. The images began to reach out for me and I began to panic. I had to gain complete control of my mind before I let the voices and faces in my head overtake me. My panic sent me into another wild rage escalating me into a frenzy that caused me to become a mad man. I soon found myself slinging books from the book case behind my desk. I broke my expensive Baccarat vases, tore pages out of the yearbook, and threw the mahogany wood finished box with the lock on it on the floor. The lock broke open and instantly released its contents of mass destruction. The handgun I kept for protection was no longer out of sight. Its silver handle sparkled even in the dimly lit room catching my eye as it seduced me to pick it up. My hands shook as I stroked its shiny barrel. My cries to the Lord had been unanswered, but here was a way out and a solution. One quick pull of the trigger and my pain and suffering would come to an end. The pain of my reality joined forces with the images of my past, and both were racing at full speed towards me.

I used both hands to steady my hold on the gun as I raised it to the temple of my head. There was a loud banging coming from the reception area, but I didn't pay it any attention, and I continued to hold the gun and placed my finger on the trigger. The banging on the door grew louder, but I still did not let the gun go from my head. Suddenly there was a loud thunderous sound and the room and my world became dark, cold, and blank.

Chapter 16

ANOTHER DAY HAD BEGUN, BUT I could barely recall the last events of the day before. I was awakened by a sharp pain in my abdomen, followed by a slow yet steady thumping in my head. I tried to regain my focus, but could not for the life of me figure out where I was. My mouth went dry as I tried to speak out. Though I was lying down, I wasn't able to move as much. Every time I tried to arise, the pain would arrest my attempts, and force me back down again. I felt dizzy and disoriented, and became frustrated at my lack of control. My eyes finally began to focus on my surroundings and although I had no idea how I got there, I began to recognize that I was in a hospital. Muggy objects suddenly became familiar as I also came to realize I was not in the room alone. I could feel the soft strokes across my forehead and recognized it was my mother's gentle touch.

When my eyes met hers, she began to smile as relief began to take over her worry. My mind was fully conscious. But words were still stuck somewhere between my throat and my mouth. She patted me against my chest to reassure me that everything was going to be just fine. She answered my question even though I wasn't able to ask it. "It's okay, baby. You're in the hospital. Just take it easy son." I closed my eyes and tried to relax. I needed to remember what happened.

"Dr. Phillips? Can you hear me Dr. Phillips? If you hear me, squeeze my fingers once," a voice called to me. The voice called again but this time it seemed a lot closer. I obeyed the command and squeezed the fingers that were forced in my hand. My grip was weak but it seemed to appease the voice. My eyes were finally in focus and the pain in my abdomen had diminished to dull, yet incessant ache. The voice continued and I was able to understand its coaching.

"Dr. Phillips, I'm Dr. Paul Warren. I was assigned to your case after they brought you up to the emergency room last night. That was quite a nasty accident you had."

"I'm not sure what happened," the words finally made their way out of my mouth. "Last thing I remember I was in my office."

"Yeah that's where the lady said she found you," Dr. Warren said.

"What lady are you talking about?" I asked.

"I assume she is a close acquaintance, she stayed most of the night. I think your mother finally convinced her to go home to get some rest a few hours ago."

"I can't seem to place any of what you are telling me." My voice trailed off as I squeezed my eyes shut, trying to let my memory aide as a compass.

"Sir, don't worry about your memory because it all will come back to you soon. It's probably a side effect from the alcohol. The bookcase behind your desk also fell on you somehow. It seems that the young lady had the security officer break in your office, after she heard a crash from the reception area. When they finally did get in your office the bookcase had fallen on top of you. You were pinned underneath it for a while. The paramedics and rescue squad were able to lift it to get you from underneath. I'm just going to do a routine check of your reflexes to make sure there is no more damage or paralysis. Tell me can you feel this?" Dr. Warren performed the routine tests and concluded there were no permanent internal damages.

"Well as far as I can tell, everything checks out. We took x-rays and you did crack a couple of ribs. But with time, they'll heal and shouldn't pose any problems. You'll have to take it easy for awhile. Maybe take some time off for a couple of weeks. You were lucky, my friend. This could have been a real tragedy."

"When can I go home?" I was anxious to get up even though I felt like hell.

"Dr. Jackson stay here another day and we will see about releasing you tomorrow sometime. You'll have to limit your daily activities for awhile, and get some bed rest for the next couple of days. I am going to give you something for the pain and something to help you sleep as well. Other than that you should be back to your old self in a couple of weeks, a month at the most. I have talked enough. I am going to get out of the way here and let all those people who have been waiting to see you come inside now."

Dr. Warren left a trail of "Thank you and God bless you," behind him. Darren, Tanya, and Brian walked in carrying their worry and concern on their faces. Darren tried to be cool but I could see his concern through the nonchalant mask he was wearing. Everyone was in the room but there was no Denise in sight. The nervous shatter seemed to fade as I went in and out of consciousness. The medicine relaxed not only my muscles but the tightness in my head. I tried to stay present, but soon I was boarding a flight to "la-la-land" and gladly took my seat and buckled up for the ride.

Just as Dr. Warren had predicted, my memory began a slow ascension back to my consciousness. The events the night before took center stage as my dreams transformed what happened right before the bookcase fell. There were flashes of silver shooting around the room that was shrouded in total blackness. I could feel a cold hard object pressed at the right temple. The flashes were fast and repetitious, and the cold metal pressed to my brain, which sent chills all over my body. The image played over and over, and then ended with a sudden bang, that jerked me straight up in the bed. The pain surged in my abdomen as a reminder of where I was. I sank back into my sweat drenched pillow and screamed out loudly in pain. There was a low whisper in the room that was soon interrupted by my outburst. When I finally was able to allow my eyes to focus much clearer there she was standing on the other side of the room. Denise was standing in the far corner. She had been kneeling but was startled to her feet when I yelled as loud as I did.

"You scared me! Are you doing okay? Do you want me to go get someone?" Denise sprang into action as she fumbled around my head looking for the call button.

"Denise I'm okay. Really I am Denise! I guess I was dreaming. It was like something had me by my head and then there was this noise..." I made myself stop wanting to tell her any of the details of my dream.

"It is good to see that you are up now! I know you need your sleep and all, but seeing you sleep like that without moving a muscle was creeping me out. Your arms all crossed over your chest like you dead. I was about to come over there and shake you, or poke you." She laughed.

Her tone made me laugh but my ribs didn't find her jokes that funny. The pain mingled with laughter as I tried to recess both.

"I'm sorry. I guess it hurts to laugh, huh? How are you feeling? You ready to run?" She quipped. Her smile was infectious and her eyes captivated me. There was a calmness that subdued me whenever I looked at her that eased me into submission. I wanted to talk a lot just to keep her talking to me so that I could drown myself in her comforting tone. Her words flowed effortlessly as she seemed to know when to be light and when to be serious. She sat carefully on the edge of the bed at first and I motioned for her to sit closer.

"It's alright," I assured her as she moved over to me. A well respectful silence fell between us that was not awkward. It was instead spontaneity that acknowledged the moment to be tender yet unspoken, and understood without the description of words. She drew her face close to me and leaned in and said, "You scared the hell out of me Jay!" Her candidness took me by surprise, and I laughed and cried out of pain all at the same time. I broke through her apologies with, "You trying to kill me! Security!"

We both laughed as I held my stomach tightly. Denise tried to calm me down but her, "I'm sorry, I'm sorry. Ooh Jay don't make me laugh, don't laugh. Okay I'll stop. I'm sorry," did not help me suppress the laughter. We calmed down and surrendered to how good it was to share a great comic relief. Most people would have said that this was no time to be joking around the way we were. However, Denise knew just how to ease me when I was tense. She also knew she could get anything out of me if I didn't feel defensive or threatened. "Jay on the serious side, I'm glad you're a little better. When I saw you under that bookcase, I didn't know what to do. That security guard radioed for help and they managed to get you out. I was a basket case. One of the paramedics tried to get me to leave the room, but I promised him I would pull it together."

"I can't imagine how that must have looked. I got pretty wasted. You know I can't hold my liquor!" I smiled hoping she would smile too. I felt the need to avoid any hard questions but knew she wouldn't let me get away with it. Denise described what the room looked like and how destroyed it was. I sat and listened but allowed my mind to stray off for a minute or two. The gun had not been mentioned by anyone, and I couldn't figure out what happened to it. I thought the loud noise I heard was the gun going off. Apparently it didn't because the bookcase fell on me, and knocked the gun out of my hands. But where was it? "Jay, I went back to your office this afternoon to try and clean things up a bit.

Darren was going to come with me but he wanted to see you first. So I went by myself to get started. I'm sure everyone's been asking you what's wrong. And I got a pretty good idea what started all of this drinking and disappearing. But Jay you have to talk to me. What's wrong with you?" She had not been turned away by my futile attempt to avoid the obvious.

"Ah, Denise it was just stupid that's all. Just a stupid way to react to everything. I mean...you know I don't touch brown liquor. But just everything just got all...I just got caught...just caught up..." My words didn't make much sense to me but I was hoping that they would get past her somehow. They didn't, and she continued her line of questioning.

"Jay, don't do that! Don't try to avoid or delay with the excuses you giving me right now. Look," she walked over to the chair in the corner and snatched open her purse, and then she returned to the side of the bed where I was sitting. She reached inside her purse and pulled out the gun. "I found this close by you when they lifted the bookcase off of you. Luckily no one else saw it and I hid it in my purse before anyone could see it." She repeated her action tucking the gun back in her purse. We both became silent for different reasons. I was searching for a quick way out of a suddenly sticky situation. And Denise was determined to get some real answers.

"Don't worry, it's legal. I bought that when I had that psychotic patient I treated a while back. I may be professional, but I am not a dummy. That guy was crazy!" I paused for laughter, but it never arrived.

131

"I bought it for protection…the gun is registered so there is no need to worry."

"I'm not worried about the law Jay, I'm worried about you. What was it doing out?"

"I kept it in a box with a lock. I guess it must have fallen out when the shelf fell." I leaned on all hope thinking that will end her line of questioning. She probed some more, but not with direct questions. Instead she drew her own conclusions from what seemed obvious, and she prepared her words for a direct confrontation.

"Jay, don't try and play me. It was lying awfully close to you. A little closer than a coincidence I would say." She paused for a moment to look directly. Her gaze begged for answers. Answers I wanted to give her, but I couldn't find a way to explain.

"Things have been so messed up, especially these last few days. I left the house initially just to get away and collect my thoughts. It's ironic that people come to me to help them find the answers to all of their problems. But I can't seem to even help myself. I got a call about what happened to Jason, and I just felt like a complete failure. All he ever wanted was someone to care about him and to listen to him. It seems here lately I have done a great job in disappointing everyone. The whole time I was in my office I kept hearing all these voices in my head. I can now remember how cold the handle felt, and I could actually see the bullets in the chamber. I heard pounding coming from the outer office, and next thing I knew everything was blank. I'm not sure if I really would have pulled the trigger, but at the time I was out of control."

Denise glanced back down at her purse and paused before looking up towards me again. She had regrouped, and I could see from the expression on her face she was ready to tell me how she really felt.

"You know in all the time since we broke up, I have had to sit in the shadows and just take it all in. Jay I can't pretend like I know what you may be going through right now, but that doesn't excuse you from holding back so much from me. See, I knew I deserved to be happy, and I know that one day the right man would come along. Jay I prayed and hoped that the someone I always wanted would be you. I just don't think you have the right to claim all this misery you've been calling yours. You have the love of God, your family, your friends, and more importantly you have me in your life.

"Denise I'm crying out to God everyday," I interrupted, "I am crying out as loud as I can. But look where praying has gotten me! I am laying here with my ribs all broken and I am worst off than I was before." My anger flared up but the pain of my injury flattened me back down in the bed. The fury engulfed me as I began to curse in rapid succession.

I was enraged and frustrated with my newly found disability. The tears returned, and I turned away from Denise's face. I was angry with her for making me think about God and my relationship with Him. I finally got the strength to turn back around to Denise as she was walking towards the door to leave.

"I have tried to trust in God Denise. But no one ever came to my rescue. No one! I am standing in my office with the gun right next to my head, and I tried and tried to end it all. But Denise all that happened to me is a damn bookcase fell on my head." I continued to scream and my rage took us both by surprise. Denise finally opened the door to leave, but before she walked away she paused for a minute. As Denise looked at me it seemed as though this would be the last time we would ever talk. I whispered I am sorry, but I did not get a response back from her. As I walked over by the window to escape it all she turned to me and said, "Jay, it was God who allowed the bookcase to save your life."

Acknowledgments...

I WANT TO FIRST THANK God for making this nine-year dream come into fruition. You have given me the ability to allow my words to flow from my head and now into this book. I decided that I would not name anyone in my acknowledgments. Everyone reading my novel has contributed to my success be that through a supportive fan, family member, close friend, acquaintance, or an associate.

I have learned that the inconsistency of Man is not to be trusted. That is why I chose not to name anyone. This way no one who is just entering my life, departing from my life, or still in my life, will feel that he or she has not been publicly acknowledged. If you are someone who is dear to me I have already told you privately the way I feel about you.

I want to thank the following: every college/university, my literary mentors, the media at large, various national art and literary festival directors, book clubs, my editors, my publishing company, civic groups, my past and former spiritual advisors, local Atlanta, Florida, and New York churches, my publicist, my two assistants, my legal staff, and my A' team members.

A few hurtful experiences birthed this novel, Behind His Mask. Letting go of my past and yielding to a better future gave me the strength and courage to share Jackson, Denise, and Darren with all of you. Remember to thy own self be true. Love has to start from within you. Then and only then will you understand loves power, its depth, and its meaning. I had to go through nine years of pain, suffering, disappointments, and bad romantic and platonic relationships to be where I am today. It was not until I gave God a yes, that I was able to focus and publish this book. Follow your dreams, conquer your valley's, and dare to be different. Thank you all for reading my novel, and I hope you have as much fun reading this book as I have had writing it all these years. Jackson, Denise, and Darren's story is now sent into the world. Enjoy!

Sincerely,

Mr. D. J. Coleman
-2009-

17396185R00083

Made in the USA
San Bernardino, CA
13 December 2014